The Flying Carpet Thief
The Fifth Case

Also by Sally Gardner

1. Operation Bunny
2. Three Pickled Herrings
3. The Rollercoaster Case
4. Matchbox Mysteries

THE MAGICAL CHILDREN SERIES

The Boy with the Magic Numbers

The Invisible Boy

The Boy with the Lightning Feet

The Boy Who Could Fly

The Smallest Girl in the World

The Strongest Girl in the World

Lucy Willow

For Older Readers

I, Coriander

The Red Necklace

The Silver Blade

The Double Shadow

The Flying Carpet Thief
The Fifth Case

Sally Gardner

ORION CHILDREN'S BOOKS

This edition published in Great Britain in 2017 by Hodder and Stoughton

3 5 7 9 10 8 6 4 2

A CIP catalogue record for this book is available from the British Library.

ISBN 978 1 44401 016 9

Printed in Great Britain by Clays Ltd, St Ives plc

The paper and board used in this book are from well-managed forests and other responsible sources.

Orion Children's Books
An imprint of
Hachette Children's Group
Part of Hodder and Stoughton
Carmelite House
50 Victoria Embankment
London EC4Y 0DZ

An Hachette UK Company
www.hachette.co.uk

www.hachettechildrens.co.uk

To my amazing brother Charlie.

With all my love,

SG

Chapter One

George Murray-Mooney had been sent to his room with no tea and no telly. It was a fate that often befell George. At the tender age of seven he could do nothing right, whereas his sister Josephine, aged six months, could do nothing wrong. It seemed unfair. He had been asking for a brother for ages and he had waited patiently, only to find out he had a baby sister. When George grew up he was going to change the law so that children were asked if they wanted a sister or a brother. It was far too important a decision for parents to make on their own. And Josephine was the stupidest name that his mum and dad could have chosen from the whole book of names.

Anyway, what use is a baby? It can't play, it's sick all the time, it cries, and it makes your very loving mum turn into a dragon.

That's what George Murray-Mooney thought as he made his way to his bedroom – rather slowly, in the hope that his mum might realise that he was not to blame. Not this time. He hadn't touched his sister and the jam in her hair wasn't his doing.

'George,' his mum growled from the kitchen. 'Bedroom.' That was when George happened to glance into the sitting room. His mum had moved the furniture to one side so that the old Persian carpet could be rolled up and taken to the oriental carpet sale the next day. What George saw made him look again. The Persian carpet was moving. In fact, it was hovering gently back and forth above the wooden floor as if it was building up steam.

'Mum!' shouted George. 'Come quick – come and see what the carpet is doing.'

'George,' said his mum, her voice stern over the wails of his little sister. 'Do I have to take you to your room myself?'

'No,' said George. 'I just thought you might like to know what's going on.'

At that moment the carpet began to edge its way towards the French windows, which had been opened to let in the spring air. George decided something must be done. He would stop the carpet from leaving. Mum would be pleased and he might be allowed to watch telly after all. He sat down firmly on it.

'George,' shouted his mum again. 'Why aren't you in your bedroom?'

'Because,' said George, 'the carpet . . .'

But he didn't finish what he was saying, for the carpet and George flew out of the French windows and down the garden path. It looked as if they were about to crash into the shed when the carpet, with George holding on tight, soared into the teatime sky. Below, his mum waved frantically at him. George waved back.

This, he thought, is much better than being sent to bed with no tea and no telly. This is a proper adventure.

Chapter Two

A week earlier, Mr Flower, the manager of the Red Lion Hotel in Podgy Bottom, had thought nothing of it when the ballroom was booked by a Mr Omar Enzo for a carpet event. It wasn't unusual for the hotel to rent out the ballroom to people wishing to put on craft fairs, or exhibitions by local artists, or a Christmas bazaar. He didn't bat an eyelid when he saw the publicity flyers: **NEW ORIENTAL CARPETS FOR OLD** printed in purple on yellow paper.

It was, thought Mr Flower, as he munched on a carrot, just a gimmick to pull in the punters.

'Well,' said Joan, the receptionist, 'nothing can go wrong with an oriental carpet sale, can it?'

'Definitely not,' said Mr Flower, his nose twitching. After what had happened at the Hallowe'en Ball last year with the mad purple rabbit and the electronic Scary Chicken Legs, the last thing the Red Lion Hotel needed was any more drama. 'I mean, a carpet is a carpet and that's all there is to it.'

'You're right,' said Joan. But she was less sure. 'Unless it's a flying carpet.' She let out a nervous little laugh and quickly added, 'Which of course, it isn't.'

The day that George was swept off on a magical carpet ride, the phone at the hotel reception desk hadn't stopped ringing. Everyone had wanted to know if Mr Omar Enzo was serious about his offer of new oriental carpets for old ones.

'I have a carpet that the cat was sick on – do you think Mr Enzo would swap it for a new one?'

'My dog has chewed the corners of our Persian rug – do you think Mr Enzo would swap it for a new one?'

'I have a carpet that my grandfather bought in Morocco and we've kept it in the garden shed – do you think Mr Enzo would swap it for a new one?'

'I'm sorry but I don't know,' said Joan.

She phoned Mr Omar Enzo to ask if he really meant that all old oriental carpets would be swapped for new ones, no matter what state they were in.

'Any oriental carpet will be perfectly welcome,' he said.

By teatime that afternoon Joan couldn't wait for the whole thing to be over. The only trouble was that the sale was due to start at eleven o'clock the following day, but so far there had been no sign of Mr Omar Enzo or his carpets. Usually people arrived well in advance to transform the ballroom into an art gallery or craft fair. Joan was in a terrible state. She'd tried to phone Mr Enzo again but without success.

Mr Flower was staring idly out of his office window when Joan rang him. It was then that he stopped looking out of the window, which was a pity, because otherwise he would have seen George Murray-Mooney landing in the hotel car park on a flying carpet. He would also have seen the carpet forming itself into a step at one end and George climbing off and watching the carpet whizz up into the air without him.

'What shall we do if Mr Enzo never turns up?' asked Joan.

Mr Flower turned back to the view from his window for inspiration and noticed a small lad waving at something in the sky.

'Joan – I'll ring you back,' said Mr Flower. He opened his window. 'Is everything OK?' he called to the boy.

'Yes,' said George.

'Where's your mother?'

'At home,' said George.

'Did you come with your father? Is he a guest of ours?'

'No,' said George. 'I came on a flying carpet.'

'How charming,' said Mr Flower and went out to collect the lad.

Twenty minutes later, Mrs Murray-Mooney was reunited with her son.

'It wasn't my fault,' said George. 'The carpet just took off through the French windows.'

'He has a very vivid imagination,' said Mr Flower.

Mrs Murray-Mooney was so pleased to see her son safe and sound that she thought better of saying she had seen him take off. After all, who would believe her? Such magic belongs in fairy tales.

Chapter Three

Emily Vole noticed that something wasn't right. No, something was decidedly wrong. She wasn't sure if it was even possible, but somehow a small grey cloud had found its way into Wings & Co, the famous fairy detective agency, and was hovering near the ceiling above the curious cabinets. Every now and again it turned from a whitish grey to a darker grey that threatened rain.

Emily Vole had been left Wings & Co by the late Miss Ottoline String. It was Miss String's wonderful cat Fidget, a tortoiseshell cat, one hundred and eighty-three centimetres tall with a very good taste in clothes, who had rescued Emily from the dreadful Dashwoods.

But that was all in the past. These days Emily lived happily with Fidget, a bad-tempered fairy called Buster Ignatius Spicer, who had been eleven for one hundred years, a magic lamp and Doughnut the dog. Oh, and of course, most important of all, seventeen keys, each with a pair of wings and one single boot.

Emily was the Keeper of the Keys, and occasionally, when the wind was blowing in the right direction, one of the keys might feel like opening a drawer in the curious cabinets and bringing a fairy back to collect his or her wings. But they spent most of the time lolling about, being waited on wing and boot by the magic lamp, who counted the keys among his closest friends.

The cloud looked lugubrious, which was Emily's favourite word, a word that sounded exactly like what it meant, a bit down in the dumps in a greyish sort of way.

'Are you all right?' Emily asked the cloud, not really expecting the cloud to answer back.

To her surprise the cloud started to change shape until one arm and hand appeared, then another arm and hand, then two legs sculpted from grey fluffy stuff. It went on to make a head, a nose, an eye and a mouth.

'I'm as right as a grey cloud on a sunny day can be,' said the cloud. 'Which is slightly better than a thunderous cloud but not as good as a pink cloud. My greatest wish of all is to be a grey cloud with a silver lining.'

'Do you have a silver lining?' asked Emily.

'Of course I don't. If I did, I wouldn't wish for it. What a silly question.'

'Why are you here?'

'That is an even sillier question and you know it,' said the cloud. 'It also could be seen as a very rude question. Anyone who knows me would be able to tell you straightaway why I'm here. I take it you are not a fairy.'

'No,' said Emily with a sigh. 'I'm not. I'm Emily Vole.'

'You are the amazing Emily Vole?'

'I don't know about amazing,' said Emily.

'Maybe you're right,' said the cloud. 'You can't be that amazing if you don't know who I am.'

The cloud became greyer still.

'Oh dear,' said Emily. Help was most definitely needed. 'Would you mind waiting here a moment while I go upstairs and fetch Fidget?'

'I was wondering when you would get to the point instead of wafting about with no reason at all. It's Fidget I am here to see.'

Upstairs in the sitting room Fidget was shopping online and he wasn't best pleased to be interrupted.

'Not now, my little ducks.'

'This is important,' said Emily. 'I think you should come down to the shop.'

Fidget clicked on the 'Buy' button before he meant to.

'Buddleia and bindweed,' he said. 'That's done it. We'll just have to see what turns up.'

'A cloud,' said Emily. 'That's what's turned up and it's inside the shop, threatening to rain. And asking for you.'

'What colour cloud?' asked Fidget gravely.

'Grey,' replied Emily.

'Grey, very grey, slightly grey or near thundery grey?'

'There is something of an April shower about it, if you see what I mean,' said Emily.

'I prefer pink clouds,' said Fidget, following Emily down the stairs. 'All pink, not a smidgen of grey.'

The cloud sat cross-legged on the counter, gathering wisps of itself to keep its shape together.

'Bad news?' asked Fidget.

'Greyish,' said the cloud.

It rummaged inside its fluffy folds before bringing out a letter.

'You're a postman,' said Emily.

'Do you try to teach her?' the cloud asked Fidget. 'Or is she as hopeless as she appears?'

Fidget wasn't listening. Neither was Emily. The letter was addressed to him and stamped on the envelope were the words VERY VERY VERY URGENT.

Chapter Four

Fidget was many things, but the one thing he wasn't was secretive – or he never had been up to now. He took the letter to his bedroom to read and Emily heard him lock the door. When he didn't come down for tea, Emily took his up to him.

'I've made you some fish paste sandwiches,' she said.

'Later, my little ducks,' called Fidget.

Emily could hear that he was on the phone. She longed to put her ear to the door and listen to what he was saying, but that wouldn't be a polite thing to do. Nevertheless, she was a detective and sometimes detectives had to use any means possible to find out what was going on. This was most definitely one of those moments. The words 'secret' and 'tatton' seeped out, and 'fading', a word Emily heard again and again. None of it made any sense to her.

'Crikey,' said Buster, when Emily returned to the kitchen. 'It must be serious. That's his favourite fish paste.'

That evening Fidget was very untalkative and just fiddled with his fish fingers in a half-hearted manner. Emily thought it felt as if the grey cloud was still in the shop.

'Please tell me what's going on,' she said.

'Nothing, my little ducks, nothing you need worry about.'

And that was all Fidget would say.

Emily noticed that he spent an hour in the bathroom that night and when he came out he looked very clean and his fur was all fluffy.

Emily had a fluttery feeling in her tummy. She went to see the magic lamp. It was sitting near the fire with the seventeen keys, who were warming their boots.

'Why is Fidget like this?' she asked, and was surprised by how weepy the question made her feel.

'Oh, fleas, I expect,' said the magic lamp. 'All that fur is enough to get anyone down.'

'No,' said Emily and sighed. 'Something is going on.'

Next morning the sky was blue and the shop was flooded with early spring light. In the kitchen, the magic lamp had placed a bunch of daffodils on the red-checked tablecloth. Buster, his hair sticking out the top of his head was sleepily eating cereal. Then, to everyone's surprise – but not so much to Emily's – Fidget arrived in the kitchen wearing an overcoat of the finest cashmere, spats, gloves and a very becoming scarf. None of that worried Emily in the slightest – Fidget was the best-dressed cat she knew. No, what worried them all was the suitcase he was carrying.

'I'm off,' said Fidget.

'No,' said Emily. Her heart seemed to be doing a warning dance. 'No, you can't leave me, you said you would never leave me.'

'It's just a short business trip and I will be back in . . . a day or so. Lettice Lovage, the dear old cod, is taking some holiday and is coming to look after you.'

'Oh no,' said Buster. 'Not Aunt Lettice!' Buster's aunt was a very powerful fairy whose day job was working as a tea lady in the Houses of Parliament. National crises were often resolved by her timely arrival in the Prime Minister's office with a plate of brandy snaps. 'Anyway, I don't need anyone looking after me – I'm over a hundred years old.'

'I'm not,' said Emily.

A single tear strayed down her cheek.

There was a clunking sound upstairs.

'What's that?' said Fidget.

'It's just the non-fairy post,' sniffed Emily.

'Well, my little ducks, best see what it is.'

Emily went up to the shop and found on the doormat an envelope addressed to her and Buster, and a small sheet of bright yellow paper with the words NEW ORIENTAL CARPETS FOR OLD printed on it in purple. Mr Omar Enzo would swap any old oriental carpet for a new one.

How odd, thought Emily. Why would anyone want to give away brand new carpets for a load of old ones?

'Fidget,' she called. 'I think you should see this flyer.'

It was too late. Fidget had put on his hat and, as cats tend to, slipped out unseen.

Chapter Five

Emily had hardly had a moment to take in the fact that Fidget had really gone when the front doorbell rang. She opened the door to find a young man surrounded by a sea of Slugsbury's carrier bags.

'Can I help you?' asked Emily.

The young man beamed a friendly smile. He seemed rather pleased with himself for having unloaded so much shopping. 'Slugsbury's shop online turns up on time,' he said, handing Emily the longest receipt she had ever seen.

'There must have been a terrible mistake,' she said. 'We didn't order all that.'

'According to my delivery note,' said the young man, 'a Mr Fidget shopped online yesterday and here I am with his shopping today, as promised.'

'Oh dear,' said Emily. 'Then you'd better take it down to the kitchen.'

After nine trips and much grunting and groaning, the shopping took up every bit of space the kitchen had to offer.

'We will be buried under these bags if he doesn't stop,' said Buster.

There was hardly any room left for the magic lamp, the seventeen keys, Buster and Doughnut to stand. They were all squashed into the corner by the cooker. 'I mean, this is stupid, really, really stupid, there are bags here with nothing in them but jars of fish paste.'

'Stocking up then?' asked the delivery lad.

'I think Mr Fidget might have clicked the computer mouse too many times,' said Emily.

'Happens,' said the young man cheerfully. 'Sign this, please.'

Emily signed, and the Slugsbury's delivery man left, whistling.

'Where will we put it all?' said Emily.

'Magic lamp, sort it out, will you?' said Buster. 'We

can't leave it here. We will never be able to use the kitchen again. Ever.'

'Sort it out? Sort it out?' said the magic lamp. 'Without so much as a "please", or a "would you mind?" Have you any idea how exhausting magic is for a sensitive lamp such as I?'

'Please, magic lamp,' said Emily. 'If you wouldn't mind.'

'For you, sweet mistress, only for you,' said the magic lamp, climbing with some difficulty onto a chair.

The magic lamp clicked its Moroccan-slippered heels together, waved its hands, and one item after another popped out of the bags and bobbed through the air to form neat rows on the shelves in the larder and the fridge. Buster counted them out and Emily ticked them off on the receipt.

There were one hundred jars of fish paste, thirty tins of tuna, fifty-five tins of sardines, four tins of anchovies, forty packs of fish fingers, fifteen salmon suppers for two, fifty-eight packs of crab sticks and thirty packs of sprats. In addition, there were twenty packs of loo rolls and twenty packs of kitchen rolls. And one large chocolate cake.

'I'm not even that keen on fish,' said Buster said gloomily, when it had all been put away and once more there was a kitchen to stand in.

It was only then that Emily remembered the letter and the flyer.

'Goody, let's see,' said Buster, snatching the envelope from Emily.

'And there's this,' said Emily. 'It's a flyer for an oriental carpet sale at the Red Lion Hotel today. I think there's something rather curious about it.'

'Oh, that's nothing,' said Buster, letting the flyer fall to the floor. 'I've thrown away masses of those.' He ripped open the envelope. Inside was an invitation to Alex Walter's birthday party.

Alex was a human boy who had helped the fairy detectives solve the Matchbox Mysteries a few months earlier.

'That's really nice of him,' said Emily.

'NICE?' said Buster. 'He is going to have a birthday. How is that nice of him? It's not nice, not nice at all that he should have a birthday, when I've not had one in over a hundred years.'

'Shall I say you won't be coming then?' asked Emily.

'Of course I'm coming. I take it there will be birthday cake and jelly?'

'I suppose,' said Emily.

'It says there will be a children's entertainer – a magician,' said Buster. 'Oh, give me strength!'

'How many of these have you seen?' interrupted the magic lamp, who had picked up the flyer.

'I don't know,' said Buster. 'Humans are always sending such rubbish.'

'You are supposed to be a detective and yet you noticed nothing strange about this?'

'No,' said Buster, slightly unsure of himself.

The magic lamp's brass belly turned red with anger. It stamped its foot.

'This is a calamity. A calamity brought about by you, YOU, I say. Do you know what you are?'

Buster thought it best not to answer that question.

Thunderous black smoke poured out of the magic lamp's spout. Emily and Buster stood well back.

'You, Buster Ignatius Spicer, are a pain in the bottom of the fairy world. A PAIN, I TELL YOU, from the beginning to the end of your rude and selfish self.'

'What's shaken your Brasso?' asked Buster.

'This,' said the magic lamp, waving the flyer at him.

Buster gingerly took it and read it.

'So what?' he said.

'"So what?" Is that all you can say?' said the magic lamp. 'Call yourself a fairy detective? Does the name Omar Enzo mean nothing to you?'

'Oh, buddleia,' said Buster.

'Oh, buddleia indeed. I'm not staying around here to be kidnapped again.'

The magic lamp stormed up the stairs followed by seventeen outraged keys.

'Where are you going?' Buster called after him.

'To pack,' said the magic lamp.

Chapter Six

It was the morning of the sale and still Joan had heard nothing from Mr Omar Enzo. Just as she was thinking she would have to tell everyone that the sale was cancelled, the handsomest man Joan had ever seen walked up to the reception desk. Joan felt her legs go all woozy.

'Good morning,' said Joan. 'Can I help you?'

The gentleman bowed.

'Please, my enchanting lady, would you be so good as to show me the ballroom?'

'The ballroom,' said Joan weakly. Close up, he looked even more like the film star. 'I'm sorry but it's being used for an oriental carpet sale.'

'My temptress, don't you know who I am?'

All Joan could do was shake her head.

'I am the one and only Mr Omar Enzo. The ballroom, if

you please.'

'Willingly,' said Joan. 'Do you need help bringing in your carpets?'

Mr Omar Enzo bowed again.

'My dear . . . ' He looked quickly at the badge pinned to her suit. 'My dear Joan, I beg you not to worry, not to put a wrinkle on that sweet unblemished forehead of yours. Everything is under control.'

Joan felt quite dizzy, so dizzy, in fact, that she didn't notice Mr Omar Enzo politely but firmly shutting the ballroom doors, leaving her standing in the lobby wondering what on earth had just happened.

The phone was ringing and she returned to the reception desk. The hotel foyer was beginning to fill up with customers carrying old carpets, all expecting to exchange them for brand new ones. Just as she reached for the phone she glimpsed a small man with red whiskers and a red suit scurrying away.

'Can I help you?' Joan called after him, but in less than a blink of a false eyelash he was gone. It must be the stress, thought Joan. Now I'm seeing things.

Among the crowd, she spied George Murray-Mooney and waved at him. George waved back. He had persuaded his dad to bring him. George wanted to see the carpet sale for himself – not that the Murray-Mooneys any longer had a carpet to swap. To George, the word 'oriental' conjured magical bazaars and unpronounceable names. Perhaps there might be camels and an elephant or two.

'Did you come on a flying carpet this time?' asked Joan.

George hated it when grown-ups talked down to him. It was really the most irritating thing they could do. Of course he hadn't. His flying carpet had flown off, he'd told them that. George sighed. How many more years of childhood did he have to go through before grown-ups would have a proper conversation with him? At that moment the doors to the ballroom were flung open and there stood Mr Omar Enzo. He threw his arms wide and greeted the crowd with a smile that could melt chocolate.

'Ladies and gentlemen,' he said. 'Welcome, welcome.'

Joan stared into the ballroom and couldn't believe her eyes. It had, as if by magic, been completely transformed. Carpets hung everywhere, lit by hundreds and hundreds of small Aladdin lamps. The ballroom glowed golden. It was a marketplace from a fairytale. Joan was lost for words.

George Murray-Mooney wasn't. This was exactly what he had been expecting.

It did not take long for the news to spread that

the oriental carpet event at the Red Lion Hotel was no advertising gimmick. Mr Omar Enzo truly was swapping old oriental carpets for new ones. The queue was so long that it snaked all the way round the car park. When the carpet-carrying citizens finally reached the ballroom, they were rewarded by the wondrous sight of an Aladdin's cave of carpets. With an eyeglass that hung on a chain from his waistcoat pocket, Mr Omar Enzo examined each and every carpet brought to him. He put the carpet on one of two piles – the first near mountain-high, the other much smaller. Mr Enzo, with his film-star looks, a perfect smile crossing his face, then invited the carpet owner to choose a new carpet from the array on offer.

Edward Murray-Mooney, George's father, was a doctor. He rather dreaded social gatherings yet it was important to be sociable, and he was so busy talking to everybody that he sort of forgot he had his son with him. George was quite used to his dad's absent-mindedness. Once, on a visit to an old people's home, his dad had wandered off home without him and George had spent a happy afternoon with a group of ladies watching black-and-white films and eating chocolates. When a rather embarrassed Dr Murray-Mooney turned up to collect George he'd found his son had made everyone feel a whole lot better than all his medicines had done.

George left his dad talking to a rather portly, pink-faced gentleman who wore an official chain round his neck. He looked exceedingly full of himself, as if he had eaten all the compliments that had ever been paid to him. He was asking the doctor about his bunions. It was obvious to George that it was a painful subject and, feeling rather bored, he went off to see if he could find any flying carpets. It's a strange thing but grown-ups often fail to notice children and no one noticed George.

Mr Flower looked on with pride as a parade of happy

customers left the Red Lion Hotel carrying their new oriental carpets. He was very pleased that the mayor had come to the sale. It was good publicity – the right kind of publicity. Unlike the Hallowe'en Ball.

The mayor mingled, speaking only to important-looking people, but on spotting the hotel manager, he said, 'Mr Flower, who is that odd-looking character in the red suit?'

Mr Flower looked around and was about to say he hadn't a clue who the mayor was talking about, when the mayor, who never listened to anyone other than himself said, 'I wouldn't swap the oriental carpet in my office in the town hall – it's better than all the carpets here. Ha ha ha!'

Wherever the mayor went he insisted that his photographer went with him, for there was never a moment, as far as the mayor was concerned, that wasn't a great photo opportunity. Mr Flower was very flattered when the mayor suggested they had their photo taken together.

'I'll put it on my blog,' the mayor said.

Chapter Seven

Emily felt very wobbly. Fidget was her anchor; he was the best guardian a girl could have and he had gone off goodness knows where. He hadn't even left an address or a phone number. And to top it all, the magic lamp was behaving most oddly. It was now in the attic, rummaging about. Doughnut was under the kitchen table, his head in his paws.

'Oh, buddleia,' said Buster again. 'This is entirely my fault.'

'Please will you tell me what's going on?' asked Emily. 'Who is Mr Omar Enzo?'

'Mr Omar Enzo is a famous magician and flying carpet thief but I've no idea what he's up to in Podgy Bottom. New carpets for old just doesn't make sense.' Buster stopped and looked down at his shoes. 'You saw that flyer for the first time today and you knew something about it was wrong, and I saw loads of them and I didn't.'

'But what I don't understand is why the magic lamp is so frightened of this Mr Omar Enzo. Was it mixed up with him in the past?' asked Emily.

Buster shrugged and was about to say something when from the upper floors of the shop they heard a *thump-thump-thump.*

'As usual,' cried the magic lamp, 'I have to do everything myself. Me, just me, without a soul to help.'

Emily rushed up to the first floor landing to find the magic lamp, carrying a tiny suitcase and pulling a small, rolled-up carpet down the stairs. The keys were riding on it, waving their booted feet back and forth. Before she could help, the carpet gathered speed,

unrolled itself and ran over the magic lamp. The keys flew off and Emily couldn't help but think they were giggling.

'Don't just stand there,' said the magic lamp, its words muffled by the carpet.

'What are you doing?' asked Emily.

Lifting the carpet off the lamp wasn't easy.

'Oh, sweet, sweet mistress, this is a calamity, a calamity, I tell you.' The carpet rolled itself up again. 'I have to leave, there isn't a millisecond to waste.'

'Please stop and explain,' said Emily.

'No time,' said the magic lamp. 'No time.'

In the shop the keys sat in a row on the counter while the magic lamp tried to make the carpet lie flat on the floor.

'Help me,' said the lamp. 'It's being stubborn.'

Emily and Buster couldn't see what the problem was or, more to the point, why the magic lamp wanted the carpet in the first place.

'You're not going to take it to the oriental carpet sale, are you?' asked Emily.

'That, sweet mistress,' said the lamp, 'is the last thing

I'm going to do.'

Emily managed to make the carpet lay flat on the floor and the magic lamp leaped onto it with its suitcase.

'Open the shop door, Buster,' ordered the magic lamp.

Afterwards Buster regretted that he'd done as he was asked because this was where it all went wrong.

'Stand back,' said the magic lamp. 'Sweet mistress, this is very dangerous. No human should ever attempt it for fear of certain death.'

'Wait a bit,' said Emily.

The magic lamp folded its arms over its shiny belly and said, 'All clear for lift off.'

'No,' said Emily, who was standing on the carpet.

Too late.

'BEDANGLEBEJANGLEBEGONE,' said the magic lamp.

There was a swooshing sound and Doughnut barked wildly as the carpet slowly began to rise with Emily still balancing on it. Before you could say, 'Monday comes before Tuesday', the carpet took off and Emily fell down flat on it – which was a good thing, for now they were flying above the chimney pots. But she found herself slipping further and further off the carpet until her legs were dangling in the air and she was left clinging for dear life to its fringes.

'Buster, help!' she shouted. 'Help!'

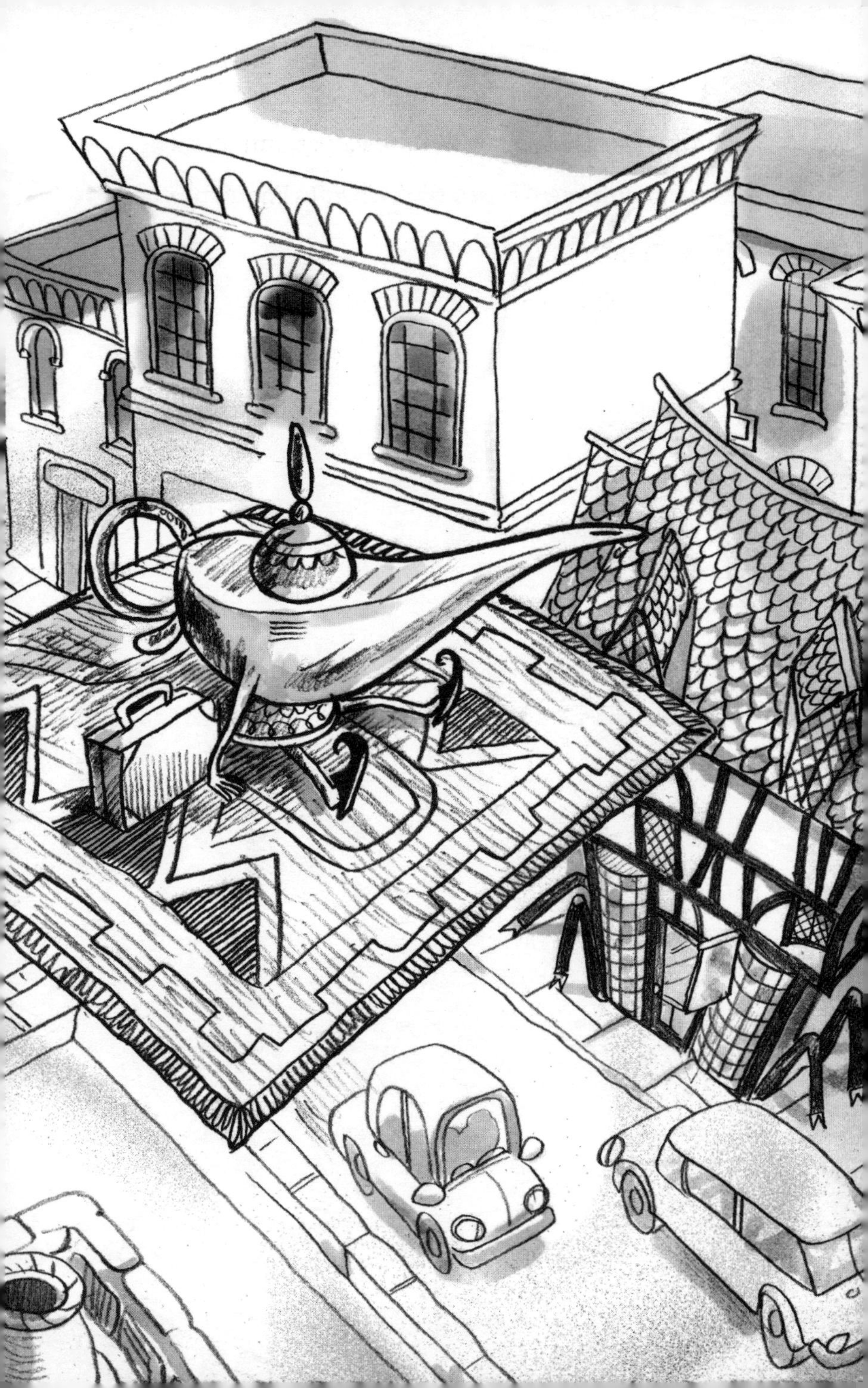

But she was out of earshot. Emily was just able to make out Wings & Co down below before Podgy Bottom disappeared beneath the clouds.

Chapter Eight

It was nearing the end of the afternoon when George saw a small, red-whiskered gentleman, not much bigger than him. He was wearing a red suit.

'Hello,' said George. 'Do you think any of these carpets are flying carpets?'

'I am sure as sure can be,' said the gentleman, rather shyly.

'There aren't any elephants,' said George.

'Definitely not,' said the gentleman. 'But I would put a goblin's coin on there being a flying carpet.'

George was determined to follow him but first he thought it wise to check on his dad. He was talking to the boring man with a chain round his neck again. When George turned back, the red-whiskered gentleman had disappeared. George asked Joan if she had seen a small man in a red hat and suit.

'Maybe,' said Joan. 'But there have been so many people coming and going all afternoon, I can't be sure.'

George decided to take a look behind a screen at the back of the ballroom and there he found Mr Omar Enzo talking to a Thermos flask.

'Come out, you useless genie,' he said, rattling it violently. 'I know you're in there. Come out, come out this instant.'

Mr Omar Enzo threw the Thermos flask at the wall. He was about to go after it when he saw George.

'This area's out of bounds,' he said and lifted George up by his t-shirt. 'Hop it.'

'Put me down,' shouted George.

'Cooee,' came a voice from amongst the shoppers. 'Mr Enzo, are you there?'

Mr Omar Enzo let go of George.

'Now scarper, and if I see you here again I will eat you up and spit you out.' He adjusted his waistcoat and, twiddling his moustache, called, 'Coming, my dear, enchanting lady,' and went back to the other side of the screen.

George was about to hop it and scarper when he was sure he heard a muffled kind of voice. It seemed to be coming from the Thermos flask. George went over and picked it up. On the side was painted a picture George recognised as the genie from Aladdin. The flask was covered in dents – a more battered-looking thing would be hard to find. George checked that he was quite alone, then quickly unscrewed the stopper, not knowing what to expect. There was a whoosh of purple smoke and a small genie wafted shyly from the flask. On seeing that George wasn't Mr Omar Enzo, his face lit up.

'Hello,' said the genie.

'Hello,' said George. 'Are you all right?'

'No,' said the genie. 'Far, far from it.'

'What's your name?' George asked.

'Tickle Featherbum Junior. I

work for Mr Omar Enzo. He treats me very badly indeed.' There was a tear in the genie's eye. 'Could you rescue me? I would be your friend for ever and ever.'

'What do I have to do?' asked George.

The genie looked nervously about him and said, 'Take me away from here, pronto.'

George heard Mr Omar Enzo's footsteps. Tickle Featherbum Junior sank back into the flask and the stopper screwed tight all by itself. George hid the Thermos flask as best as he could in his pocket.

'What have you got there?' hissed Mr Omar Enzo, coming back behind the screen.

'Nothing,' said George.

'Show me, you little snot rag,' said Mr Omar Enzo and tried to grab hold of George.

Just then George heard his dad calling.

'Georgie . . . George, come on, where are you hiding?'

'I'm here,' said George loudly, running into the ballroom, closely followed by Mr Omar Enzo.

His dad let out a relieved laugh when he saw his son.

'I hope he hasn't been a pest, Mr Enzo,' said Dr

Murray-Mooney.

'Not at all – a delightful child,' said Mr Omar Enzo through gritted teeth. 'I just wonder what he has in his pocket.'

'My scarf,' said George, pulling it out of the pocket that didn't hold the Thermos flask.

Mr Omar Enzo smiled a chocolate smile. 'Charming, charming. I do so love children.'

Dr Murray-Mooney took George firmly by the hand. 'I told you not to go wandering off,' he said. 'You remember the mayor, don't you?'

He beamed at the pink-faced gentleman with the chain round his neck.

'No,' said George. 'I don't. You said you would take me to the oriental carpet sale. You didn't say anything about talking to lots and lots of boring people.

'George!' said his father, then turned to the mayor. 'What can you do with them?'

'Teach them some manners for a start,' said the mayor, staring down at George with an unpleasant look on his face. 'And give them a sound thrashing when they are rude.'

'Time to go home,' said Dr Murray-Mooney. As they left the carpet sale, George heard his father mutter, 'The man's a barbarian.'

So it was that George walked out of the Red Lion Hotel without anyone knowing that in his pocket he had a Thermos flask containing a genie called Tickle Featherbum Junior.

Chapter Nine

'Oh, sweet mistress,' cried the magic lamp, crawling towards Emily. 'Don't let go whatever you do.'

Cling as she might, Emily knew she couldn't hold on for another minute. Just as she lost her grasp, the magic lamp bent over the carpet's fringe and grabbed her hand. But Emily was far heavier than the lamp and they both found themselves hurtling towards the ground while the carpet zoomed away without them.

'Don't panic,' shouted the magic lamp. 'There is a spell for this. Let me think . . .'

Holding tight to the magic lamp's hand, Emily closed her eyes.

'BEDAZZLEDBESAVEDBEQUICK!' it cried.

The flying carpet swooped back under them, narrowly avoiding the treetops, and they landed on it with a bounce.

When Emily opened her eyes, she and the magic lamp were safely on board, still clutching each other, and soaring up into the sky again.

'That was a close thing,' said Emily. 'Do you think we should turn round and go home?'

'I don't think we can,' said the magic lamp. 'The carpet is on automatic pilot. Oh, sweet mistress, this is all my fault. I am a foolish piece of brass, foolish, I tell you.'

'No, you're not,' said Emily kindly. 'Your magic saved my life.'

'Oh, sweet mistress – if I had thought for a second that any of this was going to put your life in danger I would have thrust myself into a furnace to be melted down for a door-knocker.'

'In my books, the pictures always show Aladdin sitting upright. Aladdin never clung to the carpet as we are doing.'

'Were any of those drawings done by fairies?'

'No,' said Emily.

'Exactly. The artists hadn't a clue. Flying on carpets is a very dangerous business. Oh, sweet mistress – will you ever forgive me?'

Now Emily was worried about where they were going. She could tell from the position of the sun that it was to the west. In a surprisingly short time they had reached the coast. Emily was feeling a little more comfortable and dared herself to look down at the waves that speckled the shoreline as they flew over the sea. Then she remembered Miss String talking about Ireland. In the Fairy Wars, many fairies had left England and gone to live in Ireland where people still believed in magic and leprechauns.

Suddenly the carpet began to descend through pinkish clouds into a misty twilight.

'No, no, no!' cried the magic lamp. 'Not yet, not yet!' It stood up and stamped its foot. 'New York – I tell you, New York!'

But the carpet had other ideas. Emily could see the outline not of a city but of a lonely castle perched on the edge of a cliff.

The carpet touched down, none too smoothly.

'Oh, the Statue of Liberty,' wailed the magic lamp. 'Oh, the Plaza Hotel, oh, the Brooklyn Bridge . . . the LIGHTS OF BROADWAY! Where are you?'

'In New York,' said Emily. 'Not here.' A fingernail moon had begun to rise. 'What are we going to do?'

'Panic,' said the magic lamp. 'Run about and panic unless this useless rag of a carpet decides to fly again.'

They both sat cross-legged on the carpet, but for all the magic lamp's BEDANGLEBEJANGLEBEGONEs it didn't move.

'Perhaps,' said Emily, 'we might find someone in the castle who will tell us where we are.'

She rolled up the flying carpet and they went in search of help. But as they drew closer to the castle it became obvious that it was a ruin.

'Why has the carpet brought us to this place?'

'I don't like it,' the lamp said, its voice shaking.

'No one likes being out in the dark,' said Emily. 'Especially . . . oh dear . . . especially when it's starting to rain.'

The only thing Emily could think to do was to look for cover in the castle. It turned out to be a huge hollow structure, but a part of it possessed a roof of sorts, and a staircase that, as far as she could tell, led nowhere.

'It's all right,' she told the magic lamp, who was shivering.

'It may be all right for you, but I'm near frozen – frozen, I tell you.'

It opened its suitcase and took out a teacosy that Fidget had knitted. The magic lamp pulled it on so that the teacosy covered its belly.

'That's a little better,' it said. 'What now, that's what I ask myself? Oh, sweet mistress, we are DOOMED.'

'Someone will find us tomorrow, I'm sure.'

It was then that she heard the sound of a door being unlocked.

The place is falling down, thought Emily. How can there be a door to unlock?

And then she heard whistling. Emily's heart began to beat faster. The magic lamp clung to her leg.

'What is it? I can't look,' it said. 'I can't! I hate these bits in films – I usually hide behind the sofa.'

'Shush,' whispered Emily. 'Please be quiet.'

The whistling grew weirder and weirder. And the whistler, whoever the whistler was, was coming closer and closer.

Chapter Ten

Just for one moment, as Emily and the magic lamp disappeared on the flying carpet, Buster wondered if he should go after them – but then decided against it. Someone had to be grown up around here and one hundred years of being eleven was pretty grown up in his book. This was his big chance – now he was in charge of Wings & Co. If he worked fast, by the time Aunt Lettice arrived he would have found out what the carpet thief Omar Enzo was up to. Yep, he thought to himself, he'd show his aunt he was a nephew to be proud of, a nephew worthy of a high-ranking fairy godmother.

Buster decided a little undercover detective work was needed. 'I'm going to pay a visit to the Red Lion Hotel and find out what tricks Mr Omar Enzo is playing,' he said to Doughnut. 'Keep an eye on the shop.'

Buster had put on his mac and dark glasses and closed the shop door before he realised he'd forgotten his trilby hat. He ran back inside for it and left again. But this time he forgot to close the shop door behind him.

The foyer of the Red Lion Hotel was stuffed full of people, but nothing looked that out of the ordinary. Buster pulled the brim of his hat down. He couldn't see anyone who looked like Mr Omar Enzo but then he wasn't sure quite what Mr Omar Enzo looked like.

A rather pompous man was saying, 'My dear Ray, I told you – stop worrying. I am, after all, the mayor, and a nod and a wink from me will do the trick.'

'Excuse me,' said a young man with a clipboard to

Buster. 'I'm a TV reporter. With the council elections coming up, we're doing a piece for the six o'clock news about children's involvement in local politics.'

'I'm busy,' said Buster.

'Really? It's just that you look so cool in that outfit. Would you mind if we filmed you talking to the mayor? It would only take a mo.'

'OK. If it doesn't take long,' said Buster, warming to the idea of looking cool on television.

The reporter led Buster to the pompous man.

'I'm the Mayor of Podgy Bottom,' he said. 'Who are you, sonny?'

Buster didn't like being called 'sonny'.

'I'm Buster Ignatious Spicer, a detective from Wings & Co, the fairy detective agency.'

'Rolling,' called the TV reporter.

'Don't be ridiculous, laddie. Now just be quiet and let me do the talking,' said the mayor, putting his hand on Buster's shoulder.

Buster didn't like being called 'laddie' either.

The human world, just like the fairy world, is a mixture

of people one likes, sort of likes, positively dislikes, and never would like, ever, ever, ever. Buster decided that the mayor fell into the never, ever, ever, ever category.

'I have to go,' said Buster and tried to walk away.

The mayor tightened his grip on Buster's shoulder, looked at the camera and smiled a smile that would make milk turn cheesy.

'I am a great supporter of the involvement of children in the politics of today,' he said, puffing out his chest.

Buster wasn't there to play games. Let them find someone else to talk to the mayor. He had things to do and this was boring. He wriggled free and that was when the mayor lost his temper.

'Come back here, sonny. How dare you walk away from me? I demand you come back here now.'

Buster turned and gave the camera a wave.

The mayor was red in the face. 'See? That's what I mean,' he shouted at the TV reporter. 'That's why the country is going to rack and ruin – because of badly behaved children. If I had my way, they would be beaten daily. It's the only way to deal with rude, out-of-control brats, and don't get me started on babies. Or buggies. Or yummy mummies!'

The camera continued to roll.

The reporter smiled. This was the best bit of live TV he had shot in a long while. This would make the headlines.

Half an hour later, Lettice Lovage arrived at Wings & Co to find it deserted, apart from Doughnut. Fortunately, Lettice spoke fluent Dog.

Doughnut was hungry, and a hungry dog finds talking about anything that isn't to do with food tricky, so it wasn't until he'd had his lunch, a walk and a poo that he remembered what had happened.

Lettice phoned the Red Lion Hotel.

'Good afternoon, deary. I'm looking for my nephew, Buster Ignatious Spicer. Is he there?'

'He was here talking to the mayor,' said Joan. 'But I think he's gone again. I'm not sure . . . it's been such a stressful day.'

'In what way, deary?' asked Lettice.

Joan told her about Mr Omar Enzo's oriental carpet sale.

'Did you say "Omar Enzo"?' said Lettice.

'Yes, do you know him? The thing is,' whispered Joan, 'when my manager, Mr Flower, went to thank Mr Omar Enzo, he found the ballroom empty and all the carpets gone.'

'Strange,' said Lettice.

'You can say that again. Hundreds of carpets, all vanished. And that's not all.'

'What else, deary?'

'There was a right kerfuffle between the mayor and Buster and a TV crew.'

Lettice Lovage made sympathetic noises. Joan was pleased to be talking to someone who understood what she was going through. At last Lettice Lovage hung up.

'What,' she asked Doughnut, 'is the flying carpet thief, Mr Omar Enzo, doing in Podgy Bottom? That's what I'd like to know, deary.'

Chapter Eleven

The whistling had stopped and the darkness in the ruined castle was blacker than black.

'My nerves can't take it,' said the magic lamp, still clinging to Emily's leg. 'I am now a gibbering wreck. This is too much for me. I have a sensitive constitution.'

'A sensitive what?' whispered Emily, dragging the lamp behind a pillar.

'Constitution. It means I am a delicate flower – the smallest thing can upset me terribly.'

'This is not helpful,' said Emily.

The whistling started again and the magic lamp suddenly let go of Emily's leg. It took a deep breath.

'I'm only doing this for you, sweet mistress,' said the magic lamp.

The tip of its spout lit up like a torch and it stepped

out from behind the pillar. Before them, they could see a red-whiskered, red-suited gentleman. He was about Emily's height and she noticed he was wearing beautiful shoes with silver buckles.

'Oh no,' said the magic lamp. 'A leprechaun. Sweet mistress, this is even worse than I feared.'

Unfortunately Emily couldn't remember what Miss String had said about leprechauns.

'Are you in the middle of a riddle?' asked the red-suited gentleman.

'I suppose we are,' said Emily.

'Of course, of course. And is that, by any chance, the magic lamp that brought all the trouble to the fairy world?'

'I have changed,' protested the lamp, marching up to the leprechaun. 'I can assure you it wasn't me that did those terrible things. I was but a vessel, a vessel, I tell you. It was the dragon's tooth! Honestly, I would never have done such a thing. Let me explain . . .'

The magic lamp didn't finish what it was saying for, without another word, the leprechaun booted it high into the air, its light still shining, and to Emily's horror it flew over the wall of the ruined castle in the direction of the cliff. Then all was darkness.

Emily was furious.

'What did you do that for? It's very, very horrid of you.

You can't just go kicking magic lamps about like that.'

'I can,' said the leprechaun. 'And I did. So there's the answer to your riddle.'

'Oh, this is ridiculous,' said Emily.

She was about to go out to find the magic lamp when the leprechaun blocked her way.

'Not so fast, not so fast,' he said. 'Did you by any charm come here on that flying carpet?'

'Yes,' said Emily.

'Did you steal the carpet?'

'No,' said Emily. 'It was in the attic at Wings & Co.'

'Of course, of course. Then I thank you for bringing it.' And so saying, he took the rolled-up carpet from a stunned Emily. 'Top of the turnip to you,' he said and vanished.

Emily carefully felt her way out of the ruined castle and towards the cliff edge.

'Magic lamp,' she called softly into the night. 'Where are you?'

'Oh, sweet mistress,' came a woebegone voice. 'Please help me – before my little arms give out.'

Then Emily saw a faint glow of a light beneath the

cliff edge. She heard the boiling sea crashing on the rocks below and her heart sank. She could just make out the magic lamp's predicament. It was clinging by its fingers. Emily lay on her tummy and pulled it to safety.

'You have saved my life! Oh, sweet mistress, how can I ever repay you?'

'By getting us away from here as fast as fast can be.'

'A very good idea,' said the magic lamp. 'Where's the flying carpet?'

Emily was about to explain when the leprechaun reappeared.

'"Wings & Co", did you say?'

'Yes,' said Emily.

'Of course, of course. And there's no dragon's tooth in that magic lamp that you're holding on to there?'

'None,' said Emily, shaking the magic lamp to show him. 'Swee-eee-eeet miss-ssss-tresss, pl-ee-ease sto-o-o-op,' said the magic lamp.

'And who might you be?' asked the leprechaun.

'Emily Vole.'

'Would that be Emily Vole, Keeper of the Keys and saviour of the fairies? You wouldn't be Emily Vole of 11, The Avenue, London, N10?'

'No,' said Emily, quite confused.

'If you are the right Emily Vole, and not the Emily Vole from London, N10, then it's an honour to make your acquaintance, I'm sure.' The leprechaun took off his hat and bowed. 'Leave the magic lamp out here and come with me.'

'Nooooo!' shrieked the magic lamp. 'Don't leave me all alone!'

Now Emily was a sensible girl. She wasn't following any old leprechaun into a ruined castle, especially not a leprechaun that had just kicked the magic lamp over a wall and down a cliff.

'I will stay here,' she said firmly.

'No harm will come to you,' said the leprechaun. 'I've heard much about you, Miss Vole.'

'How?' asked Emily.

The leprechaun stopped.

'Now, there you go asking a very good question, and it is a question with a very good answer,' said the leprechaun. 'It is a predicament. I can see it is a predicament indeed. Of course, of course, of course. You're not sure if you should come with me or if you shouldn't. You're not sure if I'm winding you a yarn, spinning you a tale or knitting you a story. Wait there.'

And with that the leprechaun disappeared again. Emily held tight to the magic lamp, which was doing its best to be brave, and they waited and waited and waited and both wondered how long a night was.

Chapter Twelve

By the time Buster returned to Wings & Co it was getting late. The old shop felt different somehow.

Aunt Lettice was waiting for him in the sitting room, hands on hips and looking none too pleased. In fact, she was looking mighty cross. Doughnut was sitting adoringly at her feet.

'Where have you been, deary?' she said, without so much as a hello.

'Nice to see you too, Auntie,' said Buster. He had a niggling feeling – though he wasn't sure why – that he was in trouble. He thought it might be best to change the subject. 'You'll never guess who's turned up at the Red Lion Hotel swapping old carpets for new. That trickster . . .'

'Mr Omar Enzo,' said Aunt Lettice.

'Yes, er, anyway,' said Buster, desperate to impress. 'Anyway, I went down there to do some detective work and . . .'

'Tell me you took the keys with you,' said his aunt.

'No, why?'

'Where are they, deary?'

'Oh, buddleia,' said Buster as it dawned on him what Aunt Lettice was saying.

'They're here. I left them here,' he said, his heart taking a dive into his socks.

'You left them here by themselves, deary? You, the great boy detective, who believes he should have inherited this shop? Who always knows better about everything than Emily Vole?'

Lettice Lovage looked like she was doing that really, really scary thing of growing taller and glowing.

Why do I, thought Buster, of all fairies, have to have an aunt who is a fairy godmother?

'I am waiting,' said Aunt Lettice.

'For what?' said Buster sulkily.

'For you, oh great detective, to tell me you put the

keys somewhere safe.'

Buster felt a moment of panic.

'They were here when I left.'

'Indeed. You left them here with the shop door open for anyone to walk in and steal them.'

Lettice Lovage was now as tall as the room.

'What you should have done,' she said, 'is lock them away in Ottoline String's old chest. It's in the safety manual.'

'I didn't think . . .'

'No, deary. That's because you have sawdust where your brain should be. And now someone has stolen them.'

'Are you sure?' asked Buster.

Aunt Lettice's anger subsided, as did her size, and once she was back to normal she pulled Buster by his ear to the sitting room door and flicked her finger at the stairs. Buster saw there were footprints on them.

'They don't belong to you, they don't belong to me. So I take it they must belong to the thief.'

'Oh, buddleia and bindweed,' said Buster. 'This is all my fault.'

'Never, deary,' said his aunt, 'have you mumbled a truer word.'

Chapter Thirteen

It was a black night, blacker than black can be, darker than dark ever was. Emily felt herself to be as low as the bottom of a rock. She would be warmer in a deep freeze, she thought, than she was here in this ruined castle. The magic lamp was feeling decidedly sorry for itself too, shivering so loudly that it clanked in a rather annoying manner. It was then that Emily heard a voice call her name – a voice she knew and loved, a voice that sounded like home.

'Where are you, my little ducks?'

It's hard to say who got to Fidget first, the magic lamp or Emily, but it was definitely Emily who Fidget picked up and hugged. Emily put her arms round his neck and buried her face in his fur and decided she was wasn't letting go of him, never ever again.

'What are you doing here? Did you follow me?' asked Fidget.

'No,' wailed the magic lamp. 'I wanted to go to New York.'

'It was an accident,' said Emily, holding tight to Fidget's paw as they walked up the stairs that led to nowhere.

The magic lamp started relating its tale of woe.

'. . . and then I was kicked, sent flying by a leprechaun and I had done nothing to deserve it – nothing, I tell you.

Well, nothing recently – I am, after all, a reformed character.'

The comforting thing about Fidget, and one of the things that made him so lovable, was that he was quite willing to listen to what anyone had to say and never say a word about himself.

He opened a little door on the landing that led to the most elegant set of rooms Emily had ever seen.

'Wait a minute,' said Emily. 'This is a ruin. There was no floor, there was no ceiling, there was nothing. Is this castle like Wings & Co where the rooms can reinvent themselves?'

'Something like,' said Fidget vaguely.

The magic lamp looked around.

'Are you sure that no leprechaun is going to come charging in and throw me out?'

'Not while I'm here,' said Fidget.

'In that case I'm all done in.' The magic lamp collapsed into an armchair. 'I can say no more.'

'That's a blooming first,' muttered Fidget.

Emily had never seen such grand rooms. This one had a tall window that looked out over the sea. Fidget showed her to a little bedroom – well, actually not that little. It had a four-poster bed and a fire burning in the hearth. He found her a nightshirt that sort of fitted and she climbed into bed. The pillows were so soft that before she could ask any of the questions a good detective should ask she was fast asleep and dreaming of flying.

Next morning Emily was up bright and early and she went to explore. She found a library in which all the walls that weren't covered with bookshelves were covered with paintings of the leprechaun.

'Are these paintings all of the same person?' she asked out loud.

'Top o' the turnip to you,' said the leprechaun, appearing beside her. 'There you go, there you go, flattering the fabric of meself. No, in a short word, no. Some are of my twin brother, some are of me.'

Emily looked again. She was about to try to spot the difference when she heard Fidget calling them for breakfast.

It was over breakfast that Emily began to work out

what was going on.

The leprechaun was called Hatton O'squiggle and his twin brother, Tatton O'squiggle, had set off on a mission and hadn't been heard of since, which went against the grain, as leprechauns are home-loving creatures.

'Tatton?' said Emily, remembering the name that had leaked out from under Fidget's door. 'What sort of mission?'

'There you go again, asking another question that tugs at the heart of the matter. My brother Tatton only ever listens to the half of what is said and the other half is all made up of his own thoughts. In other words he picks up the wrong end of the stick every time and runs away with it.'

Emily was still puzzled.

'Is Hatton's missing brother the reason you're here?' she asked Fidget.

'Sort of,' said Fidget.

'Why is that a secret? And if it is a very important secret then why did Hatton just tell it to me?' said Emily. 'That doesn't make any sense.'

Fidget looked itchy. He took a breath and seemed about to explain when the magic lamp came in wearing the teacosy.

'I want my flying carpet,' it said.

'You can't have it,' said Hatton O'squiggle.

'Don't you take that tone of voice with me,' said the magic lamp. 'I've had enough, enough, I tell you. I am not going to be bossed about by a leprechaun. I want that flying carpet and I want it now.' It stamped its little Moroccan-slippered foot. 'And if you think you can twist my metal with some sob story, you can't. I am not responsible for everyone's happy ending.'

It was Fidget who interrupted.

'To be honest, my old crustacean, I would have much preferred it if you hadn't shown up in my shrimping net at all.'

'Is there nothing the lamp's magic can do for her? Are you sure of that?' asked Hatton.

'Positive,' said Fidget.

To Emily's surprise, Hatton O'squiggle started to cry.

'We can't let her fade away,' he sobbed. 'We can't.'

'Who?' asked Emily.

Fidget sighed.

'The Queen of the Fairies,' he said.

Chapter Fourteen

The morning after Mr Omar Enzo's oriental carpet sale, a very strange thing happened in Podgy Bottom. The cloudless blue sky filled with carpets. They whizzed out of houses, flats, bungalows and warehouses, anywhere that one of Mr Omar Enzo's new carpets had been laid.

George's mum saw the flying carpets as she was collecting the milk from the doorstep in her dressing gown. She went back to the kitchen, deciding that she must have carpets on the brain. It was nothing more than a lack of sleep – after all, Josephine was teething.

George, on the other hand, was delighted when he pulled back his bedroom curtains to find carpets flying in formation past his window. Tickle Featherbum Junior and George jumped up and down as the sky gradually became darker.

'George – breakfast,' called George's mum from downstairs over an orchestra of screams from Josephine.

'Coming,' said George, and went downstairs, taking Tickle with him in the Thermos flask.

George's dad was sitting at the kitchen table reading the newspaper while Josephine screamed and screamed, and Mum looked frazzled.

'Have you seen what's happening outside?' said George. 'The whole sky is full of flying carpets.'

His dad ignored him. He was reading an article about

the mayor.

'It looks as if he made a right potato of himself – listen to this, it's priceless: "This is why the country's going to rack and ruin," said the mayor at yesterday's carpet sale at the Red Lion Hotel. "Badly behaved children. If I was in charge they would be beaten daily." What a silly fart he is.'

'Dad,' said George. 'Look.'

Dr Murray-Mooney did look and wasn't quite sure what he was looking at.

Finally he said, 'Flying carpets. I bet it's a publicity stunt put on by the mayor to win votes. It must be costing a fortune and coming out of our council tax, no doubt.'

Mum burst out laughing with relief. 'So I'm not seeing things after all,' she said.

'That's the trouble with grown-ups,' said George to the Thermos flask. He'd put it on the table next to his cornflakes. 'They never think there's any magic in the world.'

George's dad looked up from his paper and stared at the Thermos flask.

'Where did you get that broken thing from?' he asked.

'It's not broken,' said George. 'It's a little battered, that's all. It's had a very hard life.'

Just then the phone rang. The good thing about parents, he thought, is that they're too busy with their own problems to be bothered with anyone else's. As if to prove the point George's dad forgot all about the battered flask the moment he answered the phone – he was needed at the surgery.

Chapter Fifteen

Buster felt as if he hadn't had a wink of sleep. He seemed to have been up all night trying to work out who could have stolen the keys. He went over the facts: Fidget had mysteriously gone away; Mr Omar Enzo was in Podgy Bottom, and this had so spooked the magic lamp that it had panicked and flown off on a carpet; and someone had taken the keys. In the gloom of the midnight hour, everything had seemed very dark indeed. He had even wondered if he had lost his flair for detective work. Emily would have cracked this by now. But Emily would have made sure the keys weren't stolen in the first place.

'But this isn't my fault,' he had said to Doughnut. 'Emily should never have gone off like that. What was she thinking? Standing on a flying carpet during take-off, for goodness' sake. I mean, she's the Keeper of the Keys, not me. And as usual it's me who takes all the blame.'

Doughnut had become bored of listening to Buster's long list of complaints and had sensibly gone down to the kitchen to sleep in his dog basket.

When he woke, Buster was surprised to find himself under the shop counter. Aunt Lettice, in her fluffy bathrobe, her handbag on her arm, was staring down at him. She seemed just as cross, if not more so, than she had last night.

Buster stood up and looked around.

'Oh, buddleia,' he said, rubbing his eyes. 'Tell me I'm still asleep.'

'No, deary, you're not,' said Lettice.

During the night someone had slipped in and tried to force open the curious cabinets. They were a mess.

'This just gets worse and worse,' said Buster.

'I don't understand how you didn't wake up,' said Aunt Lettice.

'Neither did you,' said Buster quickly. 'I mean, if they were making that much racket you would have heard them.'

Lettice had to admit that Buster had a point. It was then that Doughnut barked.

'You what, deary?' said Lettice, bending down to listen to the little dog. 'Mmm. Mmmm. Really? Mmm.'

'What's he saying?' said Buster, who had no grasp of Dog.

'He says he saw a silver buckle,' said Lettice. 'On a shoe.'

'That's all?'

'Yes, deary, that's all.'

Buster opened the door to let Doughnut out for his morning poo. The little dog leaped up and down, barking furiously at the sky. Buster went outside and looked up to see that it was filled with flying carpets.

'Look, Auntie,' said Buster. 'So much for Mr Omar Enzo's "new carpets for old" offer. This might be our first lead.'

'Not being a detective, I don't know what that means,' said Aunt Lettice.

'Surely, Aunt Lettice,' said Buster, going back indoors, 'you could use your powers to find out who was here last night and where Fidget went, and where Emily and the magic lamp are and who stole the keys?'

'Don't be silly, deary,' said Aunt Lettice. 'You know very well it doesn't work like that. I can't go using magic willy-nilly, especially when I don't know who I'm using magic on. No. The only way to solve these mysteries is for you to be a proper detective and work out who would want to break into the curious cabinets. Any fairy worth his or her wings would be able to tell you that those curious cabinets cannot be opened without a willing key. And not even Emily Vole, the Keeper of the Keys, can make them do as she wants.' Lettice sighed irritably. 'What I can do' – she took her wand from her handbag – 'is this.'

Chapter Sixteen

'You're a secret agent?' said Emily, flabbergasted.

'Yes,' said Fidget. 'I have been on her Majesty's Secret Service for as long as I have been a cat. If there is any trouble, Her Majesty calls on me. Not wishing to blow too loudly on my own bloater, but I protected her all through the Fairy Wars and in the later years. This is the first time I have failed her.'

They were walking in the soft rain on the castle's crumbling battlements.

'Oh, Fidget,' said Emily. 'Surely something can be done?'

'I'm afraid not, my little ducks. Only if Her Majesty's wings are returned to her will she become strong again.' He put his arm round Emily's shoulder and gave her a squeeze. 'She would like to meet you.'

Fidget took Emily up a lot of winding stairs until they

reached the top of a turret. In a room full of windows sat Eleanora, Queen of the Fairies, a ghost woman, all silvery in the morning light. Emily had never seen anyone as beautiful – or as transparent.

Hatton O'squiggle was pacing up and down, weeping loudly and wiping away his tears with a handkerchief.

'Of course, of course,' he said to Fidget. 'It won't be long now, it won't be long at all. Of course, of course. I think it will all be over by the midnight bell. Yes, that is it, by the midnight bell.'

He blew his nose on his handkerchief. The Queen of the Fairies said not a word.

Emily, being very practical, felt that all this weeping and wailing and saying 'it will all be over by the midnight bell' was incredibly unhelpful. She suggested that Fidget and Hatton should go and do something useful.

'Like what, my little ducks?'

'For a start,' said Emily, 'let Buster and Aunt Lettice know where we are and what is going on. Tell them it's top secret. We don't want panic to spread through the fairy world, so they are to keep it quiet. And tell them that we are' – Emily had to think for a minute – 'that we are coming up with a plan. Yes, that's it.'

'We are, my little ducks?'

'Yes,' said Emily.

It was somewhat nerve-wracking for Emily when she found herself alone with the Queen of the Fairies.

She made a sort of curtsey mixed with a bow, and said, 'Good morning, Your Majesty.'

'You are Emily Vole, saviour of the fairies, the little girl who isn't a fairy herself.'

'Yes, that's me,' said Emily.

'It is kind of you to come. You didn't bring the keys with you by any chance?' said the Queen.

'No,' said Emily. 'They're at Wings & Co. I left rather unexpectedly.'

'One should plan ahead. Rushing into things is always a bad idea. Do the keys know I am fading?'

'I don't think so, Your Majesty,' said Emily. She took a deep breath and explained how troublesome the keys were and that they would never do what she asked them to do, no matter how many times she asked them.

'The keys always were difficult. We have waited and waited – ever since you became their keeper. I said to Fidget that we mustn't worry, that the keys would open my drawer, that it was just a matter of time.'

'I don't really understand the keys,' said Emily.

'No one does,' said the Queen. 'They are a riddle, as Hatton would say. Do you like riddles?'

'I like mysteries,' said Emily.

'Here's a mystery for you – do you know where my Tatton is?'

Emily shook her head.

'Then let's try a riddle. I'm full of keys, but I can't open any drawers. What am I?' asked the Queen.

'I don't know,' said Emily.

'Come on, do try. Don't look so glum – riddles are fun. I have to have some entertainment while I wait for my light to go out. No idea? Give up? It is A PIANO. Let's try another. What does a pet and car make?'

'That's easy – A CARPET,' said Emily.

'Good. Now you tell me one,' said the Queen.

Emily didn't know any, but a plan had begun to form in her head.

'We need to take you to Wings & Co,' she said.

The Queen put out her hand and touched Emily. It was a touch as light as a snowflake and just as soft.

'That's not a riddle, that's a . . .' said the Queen, but before she could finish speaking she was interrupted by the magic lamp who rushed in and threw itself at her feet.

'Gracious Majesty, Queen of the Fairies, please don't leave us!' it wailed. 'What will we do when you're gone?'

'Oh, give me strength,' said Emily, peeling the magic lamp off the Queen's slippers. 'It's awfully difficult to think with all this drama. Go downstairs and stay there while I work out what can be done.'

'But, sweet mistress!' protested the magic lamp.

'Downstairs,' said Emily.

Once the magic lamp had backed, bowing, out of the Queen's apartment, Emily returned to thinking about her plan.

'It's simple,' said Emily to the Queen at last. 'If Hatton will give me back the carpet I came on, then we'll take you to Wings & Co. I'm sure the keys will do your bidding, if not mine. After all, you are the Queen of the Fairies – I'm only a human girl.'

'No, it's impossible,' said the Queen of the Fairies. 'That carpet would never do. Hatton showed it to me. It's too small. I'm too weak to go alone, without Hatton, and I want my faithful Fidget by me.' She sighed. 'My flying carpet, the one I used to travel on, was stolen.'

'When?' asked Emily.

'A long, long time ago. It was a very special carpet. It belonged, you know, to Aladdin.'

'Who would have stolen your carpet?' asked Emily.

'My memory is fading with my light,' said the Queen. 'I can't remember . . . if only I could, I would be able to solve the riddle.'

Chapter Seventeen

Lettice Lovage and her nephew were out when the phone rang at Wings & Co. Only Doughnut heard it and, being a dog, he couldn't answer. Fidget couldn't remember the mobile number so he never got through to Buster to tell him where they were and that Emily and the magic lamp were safe but the Queen of the Fairies was fading.

Lettice didn't like to use her wings unless it was absolutely necessary. They looked a little tacky and in her book it was not good manners for a fairy to show off. She preferred to ride her old Triumph motorbike with its sidecar. To Buster, it was an embarrassment. He felt like a right sprat riding pillion wearing goggles and a helmet that were identical to his aunt's. To make matters worse, it was a helterskelter ride.

As Lettice whizzed along the streets shouting, 'Out of my way, out of my way', Buster closed his eyes.

The phone at the Red Lion Hotel hadn't stopped ringing since eight o'clock that morning. Everyone wanted to know why their carpets had flown away. Joan was already a nervous wreck.

'I don't know,' she was saying. 'I'm really sorry but I don't know.'

No sooner had she put the phone down than it rang again.

'The Red Lion Hotel, how can I help?' said Joan wearily.

She was so busy that she didn't notice Buster and Lettice standing in front of her desk in the foyer.

'For a start, deary,' said Lettice, taking the receiver from Joan and cutting off the call, 'you can stop answering the phone.'

'But . . . but we are responsible . . .'

'Stuff and nonsense, deary. What you need is a nice cuppa and a chocolate bourbon. And a little chat with us.'

Now the thing about Aunt Lettice was that there really was no arguing with her. Buster thought it might be something to do with the way she said 'deary'. It had such a final sound to it.

Joan sat in the back office with a cup of tea.

'This isn't going take too long, is it?' she asked.

'No, deary,' said Lettice. 'I just want you to tell me in your own words if anything strange happened before or after the oriental carpet sale.'

'No, not . . . oh, wait a sec,' said Joan. 'Now you

mention it . . . but . . .'

'At this moment anything would help with our line of enquiry,' said Buster.

'Well, there was this little boy – George Murray-Mooney. Mr Flower found him in the car park the day before the sale. The lad said he'd arrived on a flying carpet. It's silly . . . not important, I'm sure. But his mother had no idea how else he could've got here.'

Outside the phone continued to ring non-stop.

'Have you heard from Mr Omar Enzo since the sale?' asked Buster.

'As it happens I have,' said Joan. 'He phoned. He's mislaid a Thermos flask.'

'What's so special about the Thermos flask?' asked Lettice.

'He said it was a little one, you know, for a child, and had a picture of a genie painted on the side. I thought it was a joke and I laughed. He didn't find it very funny.'

'Did he leave an address?' asked Lettice.

Joan went over to her computer.

'You don't by chance know where the Murray-Mooneys

live, do you?' asked Buster.

'I'll check,' said Joan. 'Yes, here you are.'

She wrote the addresses down on a piece of paper and gave it to Lettice. Lettice put it in her handbag, closing it with a loud click.

'Thank you, deary, that's very helpful.'

Outside the hotel, Lettice Lovage climbed on to her motorbike.

'Come on, deary, don't just stand there. We're going to . . .'

'Pay a visit to Mr Omar Enzo.'

'Quite. Hop on.'

'No, Auntie,' said Buster firmly. 'I prefer to fly.'

Which is what he did.

Chapter Eighteen

Mr Omar Enzo's address turned out to be one of the old warehouses by the harbour. Buster was very pleased he hadn't gone with his aunt, for it had taken less than a wag of a dog's tail to arrive at the river. That's what his aunt didn't understand about being a detective, he thought. You had to be quick on your wings; you couldn't dilly or dally about the place. You needed to be on the spot in an instant, not flapping about on a motorbike.

The warehouse seemed deserted and it was covered in scaffolding. Depending on what mood you were in, it could be described as half-fallen down or half-built. He pulled on a rusty old bell, but no one answered. Thinking Mr Omar Enzo had already made his escape, Buster pushed the door and found it was unlocked.

He made his way up four flights of iron stairs until he

came to Unit Five. The door swung open. Inside there was not one stick of furniture to be seen, just a large carpet bag in the middle of the floor. Confident that no one was around, Buster went to investigate. The next thing he knew there was a rope round his ankle, and to his horror he found himself leaving the floor feet first and staring upside down at a man he could only assume was Mr Omar Enzo.

Mr Enzo twiddled his moustache and let out a not-altogether-friendly laugh.

'Little boys should stay at home and play with train sets,' he said, picking up the carpet bag.

'I would have you know that I am Buster Ignatius Spicer, the famous boy detective.'

Mr Omar Enzo laughed. 'And I am Mr Omar Enzo, the famous magician.'

'Rubbish, deary,' said Lettice Lovage, walking into the room. 'You are just a plain old carpet thief and unpleasant to boot. Now give me that carpet bag and no messing around.'

'How dare you insult the illustrious, the wonderful, the amazing Enzo?'

He began to wave his hands about as if conducting an orchestra. Buster supposed Omar Enzo was trying to do to Aunt Lettice what he had done to him.

'Waste of time,' said Buster.

'Illustrious?' said Lettice. She opened her handbag, took out a powder compact and checked her face in the mirror. 'I don't think so, deary. Illustrious means great, someone of note – not a common or garden carpet thief. Are you ready, deary?'

'Ready for what?' said Mr Omar Enzo.

She put the compact back in her bag and took out her magic wand.

'This,' said Lettice and clicked her handbag shut.

Then she started to grow. Buster really enjoyed seeing pure terror cross Mr Omar Enzo's upside-down face.

'Oh, whoops!' said the carpet thief.

Picking up the carpet bag, he ran for the door.

'Not so fast,' said Lettice.

She waved her wand and Mr Omar Enzo found that he seemed to be tied by invisible ropes. He couldn't move.

'Well done, Auntie,' said Buster, though the last part of 'well done' was somewhat lost as, with a click of her fingers, Lettice released him and he fell to the ground with a bump. 'You could have made the landing a tad softer.'

'Stop grumbling, deary,' said his aunt. 'I am thinking of a suitable punishment for a vain fraudster who cons humans out of their carpets. Warts, perhaps. Festering sores . . .'

'Please, pretty please, my enchanting lady, my supreme temptress . . . please, have mercy on me.'

'Aunt Lettice,' interrupted Buster. 'Could I do the questioning?'

'By all means, deary.'

'What are you doing here, Mr Enzo?' asked Buster.

'I am doing nothing except, out of the kindness of my heart, swapping old rags for new carpets.'

'Mmm,' said Lettice. 'I doubt that very much, deary. What's in that carpet bag?'

'You want the truth? All right,' said Mr Omar Enzo. 'I have lost my flying carpet. It is the most precious, the most valuable flying carpet I have ever owned and I want it back.'

'Where is this flying carpet?' Buster asked.

'You imbecile. If I knew that I would have it already.'

'I don't like the way you talk, deary,' said Lettice Lovage. 'You're being very rude to my nephew. I agree he has his faults, but might I point out that you are not in a position to be offensive?'

'Why are you so keen to find your Thermos flask?' said Buster.

'For my coffee, of course,' said Mr Omar Enzo.

'Really, Mr Enzo?' said Lettice. 'You must think me a fool. Now, if I remember correctly, your magic powers always needed a little help – from a magic lamp or a genie. So which is it this time?'

'Have you no respect for the great Omar Enzo's talent?'

Lettice raised her wand.

'Boils and weeping sores, I think.'

'No, no! Forgive me, dear lady,' said Mr Omar Enzo. 'Please, enchantress, free me. I will then be gone and you will never see me again.'

'And neither will anyone else and nor will they ever see their carpets again. What is in the flask?'

'Just a small useless genie. Now, please let me go. I have told you everything.'

'Come on, Buster,' said Aunt Lettice. 'You take his feet and I'll take his head and we'll carry him down to my motorbike.'

With difficulty they managed to put Mr Omar Enzo in the sidecar, his carpet bag at his feet.

'Do we really need to bring the carpet bag?' asked Buster.

'I think you'll find it contains all the missing carpets, shrunk to a manageable size.'

'And I'm not sure, Aunt Lettice, that you're allowed to drive with someone standing up in the sidecar.'

'Stuff and nonsense,' said Lettice, putting on her goggles and kicking the bike into action. 'He'll be fine.'

Aunt Lettice roared away and Buster took to the air once more, trying hard not to look back.

Chapter Nineteen

Buster arrived at Wings & Co well before his aunt. The curious cabinets looked as good as new, thanks to Aunt Lettice and her magic wand, but there was no doubt about it, the shop had the blues big-time. Buster could tell it was missing Emily. He hated to admit it, but so was he, and he was a bit worried about her too. The loss of the keys was a major disaster. In fact, it was worse than that: without the keys, thousands of fairies wouldn't have their wings returned to them. Buster could see them – the bank managers, office workers, train drivers, doctors, nurses, teachers – the list went on into infinity. They would be stuck forever, never to be fairies again. The idea was so terrible that Buster could think of nothing else.

He nearly jumped out of his skin when he noticed the cloud sitting on the shop counter, even darker than it had been when it had delivered the letter to Fidget. It was, in fact, black.

'Not bad news?' said Buster.

'Yes,' said the cloud and drew a letter from its many fluffy folds.

'Who's it from?" asked Buster.

'In my line of business,' said the cloud, 'I find actually reading the letter is more useful than staring at the envelope. An envelope never gives you the full gist of the communication.'

The letter was addressed to him so Buster opened it and read:

My dear young sprat,

Emily and the magic lamp arrived here yesterday, both safe and sound. But I am afraid we have a terrible problem, the worst I have known since the Fairy Wars. Her Majesty, Eleanora, Queen of the Fairies, is fading. Her light will go out by the midnight bell tonight.

Emily thinks if we can only bring Her Majesty to Wings & Co, the keys will see the gravity of the situation and open her drawer. With her wings returned to her, the Queen's light will shine strongly again. But the Queen is too weak to travel without her flying carpet, which was stolen many years ago. You are our last hope. Emily tells me that Mr Omar Enzo is in Podgy Bottom swapping new carpets for old. Hatton O'squiggle suspects it was he who stole the Queen's flying carpet. You must find that carpet and bring it here ASAP. Without the Queen's carpet, all is lost.

Please reply by Return of Cloud to:

Fidget,
Care of Hatton O'squiggle,
Ruined Castle,
Edge of the Cliff,
Ireland.

Have the keys waiting, winged and booted. Keep them as close to the curious cabinets as you can, just in case one decides to open the Queen's drawer.
We are all relying on you.

Love, Fidget

P.S. Nearly forgot - Tatton O'squiggle is missing.

‘I hope it’s bad news,’ said the black cloud. ‘I always like it when it’s very, very bad, thunderous news.’

‘It is,’ said Buster.

He found a piece of paper and scribbled a message on it. He wasn’t really sure what to say to Fidget. He wrote that he and Aunt Lettice had taken Mr Omar Enzo prisoner and they would make him reveal the whereabouts of the Queen’s carpet.

Buster didn’t dare tell Fidget that the keys had been stolen.

‘Is that all you have to say?’ said the cloud.

Buster showed it firmly to the door and watched as it floated away. He had to find the Queen’s flying carpet and the keys – and the day wasn’t getting any younger.

Chapter Twenty

Ten minutes later, Buster heard Lettice's motorbike screech to a halt in the alleyway. Buster helped her drag a bedraggled Mr Omar Enzo into the shop. They propped him against the counter.

'What happened to him?' said Buster.

Even Mr Enzo's moustache had flopped.

'We had a slight accident, deary,' said Lettice. 'Nothing that can't be put right. No sign of the keys? No ransom note? Nothing?'

'No,' said Buster miserably and showed her Fidget's letter.

'This is a catastrophe,' said Lettice. 'A complete catastrophe.'

Buster spun round. He was sure he'd heard a chicken squawking in the alleyway. He went outside again and found that there was a chicken sitting on the carpet bag in the sidecar.

'How did that get there?'

'Oh, I misjudged the width of my sidecar,' said Aunt Lettice. 'I had a little run-in with a lorry and the carpet bag fell into a ditch. As did Mr Enzo.'

Buster thought it best to change the subject.

'If you want my aunt to let you go,' said Buster to Mr Omar Enzo, 'you'd better start telling the truth. Do you own shoes with silver buckles?'

'Of course not,' said Mr Omar Enzo, wincing at the thought. 'What do you take me for – a leprechaun?'

'Take off your shoes,' said Buster.

'I can't,' said Mr Omar Enzo.

'Oh – right, yes. OK. Aunt Lettice, would you oblige?'

Lettice removed Mr Enzo's shiny tasselled loafers and took them up to the stairs outside the sitting-room door.

'Where are the keys?' continued Buster. 'Why did you try to break into the curious cabinets?'

'Buckles? Keys? Cabinets?' said Mr Omar Enzo. 'What are you talking about?'

Lettice returned shaking her head. 'Too big,' she said.

'I haven't stolen anything,' said Mr Enzo.

'You stole a flying carpet belonging to the Queen of the Fairies,' said Buster. 'Where is it?'

'That carpet is mine. I won it playing cards with the Queen. And if I knew where it was I wouldn't be here.'

Lettice Lovage flexed her knuckles, took her wand out of her handbag and started to grow in size.

'No – not again,' cried Mr Omar Enzo.

'We haven't got all day, deary. Where is the Queen's flying carpet?' said Lettice.

'I don't know,' cried Mr Omar Enzo. 'You must believe me.'

'Warts, weeping sores, a crooked nose – what do you think, Buster?' said Aunt Lettice. 'Hairy ears?'

'My sweet temptress, my enchanting, captivating lady – none of those, I beg of you. I want to change. I thought once I'd found my precious flying carpet I could put the past to bed, turn over a clean sheet, puff up the pillows of forgiveness, warm my soul on a hot water bottle of heroism.'

'That sounds to me like a load of dirty laundry,' said Aunt Lettuce.

'How did you lose the carpet?' asked Buster.

'It was that stupid genie's fault. I relied on him to tell me which carpets would fly and which ones would flop. On this occasion he failed to tell me the Queen's carpet – I mean my carpet – was in the wrong pile. It was in a batch of non-flying carpets that I sold at a give-away price to a dealer from Podgy Bottom.'

'Why did the genie do that?' asked Lettice, practising a few swishes with her wand.

'Out of pure spite. I gave that genie's flask a few dents to remember, I can tell you.'

'And now this little genie of yours is missing,' said Buster.

'I'm not surprised, given the way he was treated,' said Lettice.

'This is hopeless,' said Buster. 'If I hadn't got tangled up with the ruddy mayor at the Red Lion Hotel yesterday we might be in better shape by now.'

'That pompous fool,' said Mr Omar Enzo. 'I heard him

boasting that none of the carpets in my sale were as good as the one he had in his office at the town hall.'

Buster took Aunt Lettice into the corner of the shop.

'I want to have a word with the mayor,' he whispered, 'and take a look at that carpet of his. And also investigate the carpet that flew off with the little boy. That carpet never made it to the sale and it might have come back.'

'I can hear you,' said Mr Omar Enzo. 'And I can tell you it's a waste of time. Without my genie, there is no way of knowing if either of them is the right carpet.'

Chapter Twenty-One

Buster landed near the postbox on Bluebell Avenue where all the houses had a picture-book quality to them. Number 70 belonged to the Murray-Mooneys. Buster waved at a little boy who was staring down at him from an upstairs window. George waved back.

Ping-pong-ping-pong went the doorbell. Mrs Murray-Mooney answered it with Josephine on her hip. The baby wasn't half making a racket. Mrs Murray-Mooney looked frazzled and she did that irritating thing that grown-ups do when an unknown child comes knocking.

'No, I don't need the car washed,' she said. 'No, I don't need any jobs doing, and no, I am not sponsoring your . . .'

'I am Buster Ignatius Spicer,' interrupted Buster with an air of importance.

He handed Mrs Murray-Mooney a card. It read:

Mrs Murray-Mooney was quite taken aback.

'A fairy detective agency? You don't say. Here in Podgy Bottom?'

'Yes,' said Buster, 'and I'd like a word with your son – George, I believe.'

The noise that a human baby can make always amazed Buster. He could hardly hear himself think with all the screaming going on.

He said, 'What a sweet baby' and looked Josephine straight in the eye and smiled – a very rare thing for Buster to do, but this was an emergency and some fairy magic was needed. To Mrs Murray-Mooney's surprise, Josephine giggled then sleepily closed her eyes. All was peaceful.

Her mum was impressed.

'Are you here' – she looked around nervously – 'because of the flying carpets?'

'Sort of,' said Buster. 'I understand your son flew off on one the day before the oriental carpet sale. He landed in the car park at the Red Lion Hotel. Did your carpet ever come back?'

Mrs Murray-Mooney was very relieved to be able to talk about what had happened.

'You'd better come in,' she said. Once in the hall, with the front door shut, she said, 'No, no, it didn't, thank goodness. But there's this battered Thermos flask that George found at the carpet sale – he's become quite obsessed with it. He talks to it. I think it's his imaginary friend.'

George was upstairs in his bedroom playing with his Lego. Helped by Tickle Featherbum Junior he had built the Tower of London with a working drawbridge. It was so large that it took up most of the room.

Mrs Murray-Mooney went white when she saw it.

'George,' she said, her voice shaking. 'Did you really build this?'

'Well, I didn't have enough Lego and Tickle filled in the gaps,' said George. 'Tickle Featherbum Junior is good at building.'

Buster could see it was all too much for Mrs Murray-Mooney. Someone had to take control of the situation.

'Perhaps,' he said, 'if I have a quiet chat with George,

then we could come downstairs for tea and biscuits?'

'What is happening?' muttered Mrs Murray-Mooney to herself as she left them together. 'What is happening to me?'

George recognised in Buster someone a bit out of the ordinary like himself. When Buster asked him where he'd found the Thermos flask, George told him straightaway about the genie who lived inside it.

'But I've promised Tickle that he's never going back to Mr Omar Enzo and a promise is a very serious thing,' said George. 'A promise is something children don't break and adults do – a lot. Like my mum promising me I'd have a brother and instead I have a sister. I don't want a sister.'

'I know exactly how you feel,' said Buster, thinking of Emily, then feeling guilty. 'If I could just have a word with Tickle, I would be grateful.'

George handed Buster the battered Thermos flask, but try as he might he couldn't unscrew the cap.

'Oh, buddleia,' said Buster, 'that's all we need – a shy genie.'

George took the flask back.

'You don't have the knack,' he said.

He tapped the flask three times, the cap whizzed off and Tickle appeared in a waft of purple smoke.

'I don't want to leave,' he said, hiding behind George.

'You see?' said George. 'He was badly bullied by Mr Omar Enzo.'

'And I wasn't the first of his assistants to be treated badly,' said Tickle.

Buster sat cross-legged on the floor with George.

'Did you ever see your flying carpet again?' he asked.

'No,' said George. 'A small man with red whiskers and a red suit said he'd bet a goblin's coin there was one at the carpet sale, but if there was, it wasn't mine.'

'You met a small man with red whiskers and a red suit at the oriental carpet sale?' said Buster. 'Did you happen to notice his shoes?'

'They had silver buckles on them,' said George. 'And' – Tickle whispered in George's ear – 'and Tickle says the small red-whiskered man with the red suit and the silver buckles was a leprechaun, and if you were any good at your job you would know that.'

Buster ignored the insult in a noble way. After all, he now knew who had taken the keys and tried to break into the curious cabinets – it could have been none other than the missing leprechaun, Tatton O'squiggle.

'Progress at last,' said Buster. 'But I need you both to help me. Will you?'

'I'll try,' said George.

And Tickle nodded.

Chapter Twenty-Two

The Queen of the Fairies was fading fast and it seemed that nothing could save her. Fidget had sat at her bedside most of the day, remembering the centuries he had spent in her service. Buster's letter had given him some hope but now that hope was all but gone.

It was teatime, and Hatton O'squiggle had his nose pressed to the window of the Queen's Library, keeping a look-out for his brother. As he stared gloomily at the darkening sky, he saw a glint of bronze, a flutter of wings. If he wasn't mistaken, there were seventeen keys outside, flying to and fro in the rain.

Hatton called to Emily, who for the first time in her life could find no comfort in books.

'The keys! Of course, of course – the keys,' he shouted.

'Where?' asked Emily.

Hatton opened the window and the keys flew in. The magic lamp jumped up and down, kicking its Moroccan-slippered heels together.

'Come, my kittenish keys,' it cried. 'Come, my beamish brass. I have missed you so-ooooooooooo much!' Then throwing its arms wide, shouted, 'Here I am! Your brass-bellied friend who understands ironmongery in the true sense of the word.'

But the seventeen keys ignored him completely. They had come for one person and one person only, and that person was the Keeper of the Keys.

'Well, sock me in the eye with a salmon,' said Fidget, running into the library. 'What are they doing here?'

'They are here because they missed me, yes, missed me, I tell you,' said the magic lamp.

'I doubt that very much, my old sardine tin,' replied Fidget.

The magic lamp stuck its spout in the air and with its arms once more outstretched, called, 'Cyril – come to me. Rory – here.'

But the keys took no notice.

Emily stood up and the keys flew straight to her and followed her from the room. For once she felt she really was their keeper.

The magic lamp couldn't bear being left out and rushed after them.

'I will carry you, Cyril. You look exhausted after your long flight.'

Fidget caught hold of the magic lamp by its handle.

'I think,' said Fidget firmly, 'it's best we stay here and let Emily do what the Keeper of the Keys has to do.'

Emily led the keys up the twisty staircase to the

Queen's chamber. The keys stood in a row at the end of the Queen's bed and bowed their heavy heads. The Queen was too weak to talk. It was alarming how fast Her Majesty was fading. Emily reckoned it was only a matter of hours before her light went out forever. And forever was a very long time indeed.

Chapter Twenty-Three

Quietly, Emily closed the door to the Queen's chamber and returned with the keys to the library, where they became very excited and took to flying round and round the room.

'What are they saying?' asked Fidget.

'How should I know?' said the magic lamp, who did know, but couldn't be bothered to translate as its spout was out of joint.

'It would help if you would forget about your pride and thought about saving the life of the Queen of the Fairies,' said Emily. 'Time, as you might have noticed, is running out.'

'They want to go back to Wings & Co,' said the magic lamp sulkily. 'Don't worry, it's all right – I will accompany them on my flying carpet. There is a chance they will open the Queen's drawer. It is our only hope.'

'Of course, of course,' said Hatton and went to collect the flying carpet.

Emily had had enough of the magic lamp.

'When all this started,' she said, gathering the seventeen keys and threading them together with her handkerchief so as not to lose them, 'you, if I remember correctly, got furious with Buster, had a hissy fit, and without a word of explanation stormed off on a flying carpet. I tried to stop you, but you just took off without even realising I was about to fall to my doom.'

'I did save you,' said the magic lamp.

'And I saved you from falling down the cliff,' said Emily.

'Oh, sweet mistress, you are right. I have been brass-headed. Forgive me – please, please, please.'

'OK, OK. But . . .' Emily's tummy was turning somersaults at the thought of the flight. 'But . . . I think I'll be better on my own. So I'm going back with the keys to Wings & Co and you're staying here.'

'You don't mean it!'

'Yes, she does,' said Fidget.

'But without me you won't know how to get home, you won't have the right magic words . . . all could be lost. Please, sweet mistress, you need me as never before.'

Emily felt slightly less certain that she was doing the right thing, but Fidget said firmly, 'Magic lamp, another word from you and I will personally tie a fisherman's knot in that spout of yours. It's all right, my little ducks,' he said to Emily. 'Take no notice. The magic lamp is only trying to frighten you.'

'No, no,' squeaked the lamp. 'I'm . . .'

'Fisherman's knot,' said Fidget. 'Little ducks, the keys chose you to be their keeper, and you and only you must take them on this vital mission.'

Hatton was calling from the battlements.

'Come up here, there's not a moment, a minute, a second, a millisecond to be lost.'

On the battlements the rain was lashing down and the wind was blowing hard. It wasn't a night that encouraged flying. Emily put on a sou'wester Hatton gave her that was too big and a pair of goggles that had windscreen wipers. She felt like a goldfish staring out from inside a goldfish bowl.

'They will help you see where you're going, so they will. Of course, of course, you'll be all right. Keep heading in that direction,' he said, pointing into the distance.

'Hurry now, my little ducks,' said Fidget.

The wind was blowing so violently that Hatton and Fidget had to hold onto the carpet while Emily sat on it cross-legged. Fidget said something which Emily was sure was important. It was hard to hear over the howling gale. It sounded like 'soggy lot some'. Before she had a chance to ask him to repeat it, the magic lamp rushed up the steps wearing the teacosy and tried to jump on. Fidget grabbed the lamp, and without meaning to, let go of one end of the carpet. It took off with a lurch, Hatton still clinging to the other end. Fidget caught hold of his trouser leg and pulled him down as the flying carpet whizzed away, looping over the sea before heading east and into the night.

Above the wind and rain Emily heard the magic lamp's mournful cry.

'Come back, sweet mistress, come back. You don't know the magic words – without them you'll be lo-o-o-st.'

Chapter Twenty-Four

Margaret, the mayor's secretary, was having a troublesome day and she couldn't wait for it to be over. The mayor was in a foul temper. Against his instructions, the local TV station had shown his rant in the foyer of the Red Lion Hotel. It was very embarrassing, especially as he was standing for re-election in a few weeks' time.

And then there were the photographs from the oriental carpet sale. Margaret had put them up on the mayor's blog that morning but there had since been a lot of comment on social media about a little red-whiskered man in a red suit who appeared in the background of every photo. The mayor had had a fit when he'd found out.

It was very nearly six o'clock and Margaret was about to take the mayor a cup of tea when, to her surprise, a woman she recognised as her doctor's wife entered her office. Mrs Murray-Mooney was accompanied by her baby, her son and another boy.

The older lad explained that they were here to see the mayor's carpet.

'Just his carpet, nothing more. It will only take a minute or two.'

'And who might you be?' Margaret asked. She thought he looked vaguely familiar.

'I am Buster Ignatius Spicer of Wings & Co, the fairy detective agency.'

Margaret's face seemed to turn itself upside down in disbelief.

Mrs Murray-Mooney quickly said, 'I know it's a strange request, but it's to do with the flying carpets that were seen over Podgy Bottom this morning.'

Margaret's face began to right itself.

'Honestly,' said Mrs Murray-Mooney, 'this won't take long.'

The mayor hadn't been feeling quite himself since he'd lost his temper on camera the previous afternoon. He blamed that boy – Rooster . . . Booster . . . Custer – or whatever his name was. The boy probably had something to do with the red-suited photo-bomber at the oriental carpet sale too.

'If I ever see that lad again,' he said to himself, 'I'll give him a good thrashing.' He paused and took a deep breath. 'Control your temper, William,' he said, addressing a photograph of himself in his full mayoral regalia. 'This will never do. I must contain my anger. I must contain my anger,' he repeated.

The trouble was that saying 'I must contain my anger', just made him more angry.

Margaret, teacup and saucer in hand, knocked on the mayor's door and went in, a galleon sailing into battle. Mrs Murray-Mooney, Josephine, George and Buster followed in her wake.

Buster knew nothing about carpets, but even he could see that the Persian carpet on the floor of the mayor's office was special. It was huge, and the intricate pattern of flowers and birds glowed in warm crimson and gold and dark blue. There was a regal feel to it. Buster had no doubts at all – this was the Queen's flying carpet. He was already imagining flying it to the castle on the edge of the cliff and personally escorting the Queen of the Fairies to Wings & Co.

Usually politicians keep their thoughts to themselves in public. Even if they think that children should never be heard and never be seen, they wouldn't dream of saying so, but the mayor was not best pleased to see so many Murray-Mooneys, and even less pleased to see that wretched Buster boy. The mayor tried to put on a smile, the one that said, 'Ask me anything, anything at all', but that afternoon his smile wasn't sticking to his face.

What he was going to say was 'Dear Mrs Murray-Mooney, to what do I owe the privilege of your visit?' but what came out was, 'I haven't time for all this nonsense. Margaret, get these brats out of my office. It's not a crèche.'

Mrs Murray-Mooney was quite put out.

'Mr Mayor, I strongly object to your attitude towards children. You told my husband that my boy should be smacked, that it was the only way to teach children manners,' she said.

The mayor was about to say, 'I'm sure I never said such a thing, or if I did, it was taken out of context.' Instead he found himself saying, 'I hate children, boys in particular. They should be smacked regularly. As for babies, I think they should be abolished altogether.'

'I don't care what you think,' said Buster. 'We just need to have a quick look at your carpet and we'll be gone.'

It is said that red is the colour that makes bulls charge. Buster's voice had the same effect on the mayor. He picked up a folder from his desk and charged at Buster.

Buster had to jump over a sofa to avoid being thwacked.

'It's all your doing, you wretched boy,' shouted the mayor, pursuing Buster round the room. Josephine started screaming and Margaret called security.

Amid the rumpus, the mayor never noticed George or the little genie. They were under his desk looking very closely at the weave of the carpet. The security guards had just arrived when George piped up.

'Tickle Featherbum Junior says this isn't the right carpet.'

Chapter Twenty-Five

Emily held tightly to the edges of the carpet and wondered if she had made the most terrible mistake. Should she have brought the magic lamp with her? She was, after all, only human. Yes, a human who was the Keeper of the Keys, but also a human who knew nothing at all about flying carpets. Was she supposed to give it directions? How did it know where to go? Maybe she needed to say some magic words. Aladdin, she remembered, had said 'Abracadabra'. She tried unsuccessfully to work out what it was that Fidget had said before she'd taken off. If this goes wrong, she thought, and Her Majesty fades away, it will be all my fault. She was surprised to find herself wishing Buster was with her. He would be rather good at this sort of thing.

She could feel the keys wriggling in her pocket. The

night was thickly dark, a whirling cauldron of thunder and lightning without even a peppering of light. She felt as if she had been flying for hours and was completely lost.

More in desperation that anything else she said out loud, 'We must go to Podgy Bottom.'

The carpet stopped, hovered, and then turned. For one awful moment Emily thought it was going to head back the way they'd come. But just when she thought she had made the biggest muddle of everything, to her relief she saw a necklace of lights glimmer in the darkness. This gave her hope, for the castle she had just left was on the edge of a cliff with no one living for miles around.

Emily crossed her fingers as they dropped through the clouds towards toy-town houses near a lighthouse. Now they were over land again and soon the carpet was flying low along a river she recognised – it was the river that flowed through Podgy Bottom. As they flew down the alleyway where Wings & Co stood, Emily realised that the flying carpet had no intention of stopping. It was about to crash into the shop door, but to her relief the door burst open and the little carpet landed gracefully in front of the curious cabinets.

What happened next took Emily's breath away. The keys untangled themselves from her hanky and lined up in front of one of the drawers. Each key took a turn in the lock until, with the last key, the drawer sprang open. Emily was blinded by a light so bright it was as if a star had been released from prison. She had to put her hands over her eyes and squint through her fingers to see anything at all. It happened so quickly. One moment there was the most glorious rainbow light and then, in a blink of an eye, there was the Queen of the Fairies, her wings restored to her. Emily had never seen anything as magical. The Queen no longer looked pale and transparent but glorious. She shimmered, she shone, light radiated from her. If ever there was a happy ending then this was it.

Chapter Twenty-Six

Buster felt as if the flight had been taken out of his wings. The mission to find the Queen's flying carpet had royally failed. He was a stone fairy, stewing in gloom with a good dollop of self-pity on the side. So much so that he had almost forgotten that Mrs Murray-Mooney, Josephine and George were trailing after him.

What kind of fairy detective was he if he couldn't find his queen's flying carpet? And then there were the keys . . . He knew one thing: he was up to his neck in trouble. How was he ever going to explain all this to Emily? Fidget would be furious, and Aunt Lettice would have no sympathy for him. If he was honest, he really dreaded going back to Wings & Co. But the one thing Buster wasn't was a coward. He took a deep breath. He had to face the truth. He had failed.

They turned into the alleyway that led to the shop and Buster stopped in his tracks.

'WOW!' said George.

'Wow indeed,' said Buster.

'Is your shop usually so brightly lit?' asked Mrs Murray-Mooney.

'No,' said Buster. 'Definitely not.'

The windows were ablaze with coloured lights that sparkled and glinted as if stars had come down to settle in the shop. Buster had a feeling that something awesome was going on but he wasn't sure whether it was good-awesome or bad-awesome.

'You'd better wait here with George and Josephine,' said Buster. 'I'll go and investigate.'

He crept closer to the building and peered through the window. And there he saw her, standing in the middle of the shop in all her glory. Buster ran in and dropped down on one knee.

Eleanora, Queen of the Fairies had had her wings and her light returned to her. They were the most wondrous wings Buster had ever seen. Light glimmered from inside them. The Queen herself was luminous.

'Buster Ignatius Spicer,' said the Queen and held out her hand for him to kiss. 'What a pleasure to see you again. Still eleven, I see.'

'Yes, Your Majesty,' said Buster.

'It suits you,' said the Queen.

The Murray-Mooneys tiptoed up the alleyway and stopped at the door.

'Oh!' said Mrs Murray-Mooney, following Buster into the shop. She was quite overcome. 'The world is brimming with magic.'

'And you are?' asked the Queen of the Fairies.

'Amelia Murray-Mooney, and this is Josephine and my son, George.'

As George tried to say hello, the stopper flew off the Thermos flask and Tickle Featherbum Junior sprang out, clapping his little hands together.

'Oh, Your Majesty, what an honour,' he said and bowed.

Mrs Murray-Mooney had ceased to be surprised by anything. After all, so many impossible things had happened, that her son having a genie for a friend made no difference.

It was then that the Queen noticed the genie's flask.

'George, would you bring the Thermos flask to me?' said the Queen of the Fairies.

George took the flask to her and she studied the dents.

'Who did this?' asked the Queen.

'The magician who stole your carpet,' said Tickle Featherbum Junior.

'Mr Omar Enzo,' said the Queen slowly. 'The flying carpet thief. Now that my light is bright I remember everything.'

Buster was lost for words. He heard the clatter of china on a tea tray and Aunt Lettice came up from the kitchen, Doughnut at her heels.

'Now, Your Majesty, deary, this just what you need after your ordeal. A nice hot cup of tea.' She turned and shouted downstairs. 'Don't forget the cake.' Then she saw Buster. 'There you are,' she said. 'What in all the midsummers' nights have you been doing?'

'Er . . . I worked out it was Tatton O'squiggle who stole the keys,' he said feebly. 'Did he bring them back to save Her Majesty?'

'No,' said the Queen. 'It wasn't my poor Tatton. I was saved by the Keeper of the Keys.'

'She's here?' said Buster nervously.

Just then Emily appeared from the kitchen carrying the huge chocolate cake, the seventeen keys flying about her.

'Buster!' she said.

'How . . . how . . .' Buster stuttered. 'How did you find the keys?'

Emily never answered that question for at that very moment there was an enormous *bang*.

The shop door flew open and Fidget, the magic lamp and Hatton O'squiggle all landed in a heap on the floor of the shop, followed by a rolled up carpet that spread itself out in front of the Queen.

'That's my carpet,' said Mrs Murray-Mooney.

'That's my carpet,' said George Murray-Mooney.

'That's my carpet,' said Eleanora, Queen of the Fairies.

'Oh dear,' said Mrs Murray-Mooney. 'If only I'd known it was yours I'd have taken better care of it.'

Chapter Twenty-Seven

'I tell you, Margaret, I saw it,' said the woman at the next table. 'I'm not making it up. I've just seen a flying carpet heading down the alleyway – you know, the one where that funny shop is – Wings & Co or something.'

Tatton O'squiggle, the smallest, the most useless leprechaun that ever lived, was sitting in Mimi's Pizza Parlour. He had been trying to catch the eye of the waitress for the last ten minutes, but the chair he was sitting on was so low, and the table so high, that he somewhat disappeared amid

the furniture. All he wanted was an egg on toast. In despair, he had done something that such a shy leprechaun would never usually do. He'd stood on his chair and waved his hat in the air, which made everybody in the pizza parlour stare at him. The one thing Tatton O'squiggle hated – even more than semolina pudding – was people staring at him. It made him long for home and a change of socks. He'd sat down again and his eyes had filled with tears as he thought about the futile efforts he had made to save the Queen of the Fairies. It was while he was in the marshes of misery that he had overheard two ladies at the table next to him talking rather loudly. Tatton's pointy ears started to glow.

'A flying carpet?' said the first lady's friend. 'I had Dr Murray-Mooney's wife in the mayor's office this afternoon going on about the flying carpets. The mayor became very agitated and it all got quite ugly. Security called Sergeant Binns, and he tried to arrest Mrs Murray-Mooney and it took ages to sort out. That's why I'm so late.'

'Well, I saw a flying carpet. Not a word of a lie. There was a big cat on it, an Aladdin's lamp and a little man in a red . . .' She stopped as she noticed Tatton on the next table. 'Why, if this isn't the gentleman I saw,' she said, nodding at a nervous Tatton. 'It was you on the flying carpet, wasn't it?'

Margaret turned to look at Tatton.

'Oh,' she said. 'And it was you in the mayor's photographs, wasn't it?'

Tatton jumped down from his chair and, putting his hat on his head, made his escape. He ran all the way up the High Street as fast as his legs would carry him and all the way up the alley to Wings & Co. He reached the shop quite out of breath. Lights shone from the windows and he heard music and smelled chocolate cake. Finding his courage, he pushed open the door.

Chapter Twenty-Eight

The absence of the Queen's beloved Tatton had cast a leprechaun-shaped shadow over the celebration. The fact that he wasn't there to enjoy this happy moment upset the Queen and Hatton a lot, but it was late and they needed to go home. The fairy detectives would start searching for the missing leprechaun the very next day.

'Perhaps I'll find my brother at home in the castle on the edge of the cliff,' said Hatton.

The words had hardly left his lips when Tatton O' Squiggle himself somersaulted into the shop, landing with a bang at the feet of the Queen of the Fairies. Seeing his beloved queen's light restored he fell to his knees, clutching his hat in his hand.

'Oh – Your Majesty! All is well then?'

'Now you are here, Tatton, yes – all is well indeed,' said the Queen.

Hatton dropped the carpet and danced a jig. Never had two leprechauns been so pleased to see one another.

'Where in all the four-leafed clovers have you been?' asked Hatton.

'Didn't the cloud give you my letter?' said Tatton. 'I wrote that I was off to find the Queen's flying carpet. But when it didn't turn up at Mr Omar Enzo's carpet sale, I thought I'd beg the keys to open Her Majesty's drawer and bring her back to collect her wings. When I arrived here, the shop door was wide open to the world and, as sure as sure can be, the keys were nowhere to be seen. I came in and called and called, so I did, and not one word of a reply did I hear. The keys were gone, no doubt flown off.'

'Of course, of course!' said Hatton. 'They came to the castle to find Emily Vole, so they did.'

Buster was about to say he'd deduced it was Tatton who'd tried to break into the curious cabinets, but not wanting to ruin the party mood, he thought better of it.

'Let's go home,' said the Queen to the leprechauns.

'Excuse me, Your Majesty,' said Emily, 'but there is one thing I would like to know.'

'Yes, Emily dear?' said the Queen.

'Why did your carpet fly away from the Murray-Mooneys in the first place?'

'Woooh!' said Tickle, bouncing up and down, his hand in the air. 'I can answer that. Go on, let me answer.'

The Queen of the Fairies nodded.

'It's all to do with the weave,' said Tickle. 'A true flying carpet has a sat-nav thread woven into it. It's the most delicate work. But if anything upsets it, well, the carpet can lose all sense of direction.'

'And that's what happened with our – with the Queen's – carpet?' asked George.

'Spot on the fishcake,' said Fidget. 'It finally showed

up at the castle a short while after Her Majesty vanished, called back to collect her wings when the keys opened her drawer.'

'And now,' said Tatton, 'if you wouldn't mind, I need to be changing my socks. We'll say toodle-oo.'

Tatton helped Hatton unroll the Queen's flying carpet outside the shop door in the alleyway. The two leprechauns were standing one at each end waiting for the Queen to come out and step onto it, when the magic lamp piped up.

'What about Mr Omar Enzo, the villain of the piece?'

'He's locked up in the shed,' said Lettice. 'He's not going anywhere.'

'He started all the trouble in the first place, and it was due to him, Your Majesty, that I fled for my life,' said the magic lamp. 'Look what he did to Tickle Featherbum Junior's Thermos flask, not to mention my terrible treatment at his wicked hands when I worked for him. Here, see this dent . . .'

'Where is the little genie?' asked the Queen, looking around.

George was very worried that the Queen would say

Tickle had to return to Mr Omar Enzo, which was the one thing George had promised wouldn't happen.

'I'm never going back to work for that man' said Tickle Featherbum Junior. 'I'm not leaving George. He's my friend. My best friend in all the world. And he needs me.'

The Queen of the Fairies listened carefully to everything the genie said, then waved her fingers and diamond sparkles fell from them. In an instant, all the dents in the Thermos flask were gone and it looked as good as new.

'George,' said the Queen. 'Tickle Featherbum Junior will stay with you. When the time is right – and you will know when it is – then you will bring him to Wings & Co. Agreed?'

'Agreed. Thank you very much,' said George. His birthday, Christmas, New Year and any other celebration you care to mention had just rolled themselves into one wonderful moment.

Tickle bowed to the Queen and wafted back inside the Thermos flask, the stopper screwing itself shut.

The Queen of the Fairies had had a long and difficult day. She turned to Lettice Lovage.

'Lettice, I'll leave you to deal with Mr Omar Enzo as you think fit.'

She was about to step onto the carpet once more when Fidget coughed in a meaningful manner.

'Oh, yes, thank you, dear Fidget,' she said. 'I nearly forgot. Emily Vole, you have shown yourself to be a true friend of the fairy world and in recognition of your bravery I grant you one wish.'

'Oh!' said Emily. 'Thank you, Your Majesty. Well . . . ' Emily thought for a moment. 'Yes. I wish . . .'

'No, no, no,' said the Queen. 'You must whisper it very quietly to me so that no one can overhear you and you must never tell a soul what you wished for or it won't come true.'

Emily told the Queen her wish and when she'd finished she turned bright red.

'I bet it was something pink and silly,' said Buster.

The Queen of the Fairies smiled. 'Now, I really must get home,' she said.

She put her two dainty feet on her flying carpet and stood there, her wings shining as the carpet took off into

the starlit night.

Mrs Murray-Mooney and George said their goodbyes. What a wonderful world that has such magic in it, thought Mrs Murray-Mooney, as she pushed her buggy down the alleyway to the High Street.

'George,' she said. 'I know you wanted a brother, but I don't have magic powers to make wishes come true.'

'Of course you don't,' said George, putting his hand on the buggy next to his mum's. 'It doesn't matter, really. I'm sure Jo will grow on me.'

'Jo?' said Mrs Murray-Mooney. 'Mmm. It does suit her better than Josephine.'

George thought that was the first sensible thing his mum had said in ages.

Jo giggled and so did George and Mum.

Chapter Twenty-Nine

Mr Omar Enzo was looking very nervous when Fidget and Buster came to collect him from the shed. He looked even more worried when he saw Lettice Lovage waiting for him in the shop with Emily and Doughnut. Lettice was twiddling her fairy wand. 'Sweet enchantress,' he said, as Lettice released him from the invisible bonds. 'I have learned my lesson. From now, I'm going straight, my ways are mended.'

A more trusting audience might have been convinced by this performance. Mr Omar Enzo had always managed to charm his way out of any tangle. As he beamed at Lettice, even she wondered if he had changed for the better and perhaps the punishment she had in mind was a little harsh. Things might have turned out differently if at that moment the magic lamp hadn't appeared from where it was hiding behind the counter.

Mr Omar Enzo caught sight of the magic lamp, and forgetting where he was, forgetting who he was with, forgetting everything, he made a spectacular dive and landed on top of it. He grabbed hold of it by its handle and threw it at the wall, narrowly missing Lettice.

'You! You puffed-up worthless piece of brass,' shouted Mr Omar Enzo.

'That settles it,' said Aunt Lettice.

'Spot on the fishcake, old cod,' said Fidget, as he helped the lamp to its feet.

'Forgive me, dear lady. That magic lamp drove me nuts when it worked for me,' said Mr Omar Enzo. 'If you had to live with it as I did then you would understand.'

Fidget, Buster and Emily found they secretly had some sympathy with the carpet thief.

But Lettice Lovage had started to grow and she didn't stop until she'd filled the whole shop.

'I think this is going to be a good one,' said Buster.

'Dear, sweet lady, enchantress, temptress,' sobbed Mr Omar Enzo, who was now on his knees.

'Be quiet and listen. Your punishment is just and proper,' said Lettice. 'It also has the royal seal of approval. So, deary, without further ado, let's get on with it. First you will send back all the carpets you have stolen from the good citizens of Podgy Bottom.'

'Anything! I will do anything you desire, my proud beauty.'

'No need for all that, deary. Now do be quiet, I can't hear myself think. Your super-magic powers will be confiscated, that goes without saying.'

'Can I still entertain at children's parties?' asked Mr Omar Enzo.

'Of course you can, deary, but on a much reduced scale until you've learned to be kind and caring, the smile not only on your face, but in your heart too.'

'Thank you,' said Mr Omar Enzo. 'May I go now, oh merciful and generous lady?' he asked, moving towards the door.

Lettice Lovage showed no signs of returning to her normal size.

'I've not finished, Mr Enzo. There's one last thing.'

'Nothing too bad, I hope?'

'Which colours do you like?'

'I am fond of purples and reds,' said Mr Omar Enzo. 'Are you going to give me a purple moustache? I think, temptress, that could be quite becoming.'

Lettice waved her wand. Emily, Buster and Fidget gasped and Doughnut howled.

'Now may I go?' said Mr Omar Enzo.

'By all means,' said Lettice, as she shrank to her normal size. She put her wand back in her handbag and took out her compact. 'Perhaps, Mr Enzo, you would like to take a look at yourself before you leave.'

Omar Enzo never wasted an opportunity to look at the handsome features that had wooed and fooled more people than he cared to remember.

He looked at himself in the mirror and let out a heartbreaking scream. 'What have you done to me?'

Mr Omar Enzo's face was covered in purple and red spots.

'I know it looks bad, deary,' said Lettice, 'but for every kind thing you do, one spot will disappear. And be warned: for every unkind thing another spot will pop up.'

It was hard to know if Mr Omar Enzo heard what Lettice said for he dropped the compact and ran from the shop, never to be seen again.

On the Thursday before his birthday party, Alex Walters rang Emily. He was a bit downcast. The magician his mum had booked – a Mr Omar Enzo – had unexpectedly cancelled and they were left without an entertainer.

'. . . And I'd told all my friends and sort of boasted that the magician could do amazing tricks and . . .'

'Don't worry,' said Emily. 'I have an idea.'

She thought it was one of her best ideas to date.

Buster had been in such a bad mood since the end of the Case of the Flying Carpet Thief and now he was grumbling again about never having a birthday, let alone a party. He cheered up no end when Emily asked if he would consider putting on a magic show at Alex's party.

'And I thought perhaps the magic lamp might perform as well,' she added.

'Wowzer!' said Buster.

The magic lamp jumped up and clicked its little Moroccan-slippered heels together.

'Sweet mistress, I think I would be SPECTACULAR!' it said.

FIN

Look out for more Fairy Detective cases

Spot on the fishcake.

Welcome to the famous fairy detective agency, Wings & Co. There's talking cat Fidget, grumpy fairy detective Buster Ignatius Spicer, who's been eleven for a hundred years, a bossy magic lamp, and orphan Emily Vole, who was discovered in a hatbox at Stansted Airport.

Together they solve the crimes no other detectives can tackle – a plague of bunnies, some mysteriously missing luck and one very large, very lost giant.

Squat on a squid, you won't want to skip a single Wings & Co adventure.

How many keys can you spot?

How many tins can you count in the larder?